Riot Amber

a story in the
RomantiSea Serenades
series

J.D. Harbor

Copyright © 2026 by J.D. Harbor

All rights reserved.

No portion of this book may be reproduced in any form without written permission from the publisher or author, except as permitted by U.S. copyright law.

No AI Training: Without in any way citing the author's exclusive rights under copyright, any use of this publication to train generative artificial intelligence (AI) technologies to generate text is expressly prohibited. The author reserves all rights to the licensed use of this work for generative AI training and development of machine learning language models.

Ebook ISBN: 979-8-9948374-0-5
Paperback ISBN: 979-8-9948374-1-2

Cover Design: Fairchild Art
Editing and Proofreading: Mekhala Spencer, All the Proof Editing
Formatting: Nicole Kincaid, Naughty Nook PR

One

The Cherry Bomb lip gloss cut through the air in slow motion, the bright tube flashing under the stage lights as it spun toward her. Time warped around the moment. She saw it coming yet stayed rooted in place, trapped in the middle of a lyric with her guitar held against her like a shield that could not help her.

The impact came with a wet smack against her left cheek, the tube bursting open on contact. Bright red exploded across her skin, mixing with the mascara already streaking down her face in black rivulets. The crowd roared … breaking glass and shattering dreams, and more objects flew through the spotlight glare. Bottles. Programs. A platform boot?

Her voice cracked, and the words died in her throat. "Only posers fucking—"

The microphone squealed with feedback as a monstrous hand grabbed her shoulders, pulling her backward. Security. Black shirts. Urgent voices cutting through the chaos.

"We need to get you out of here NOW!"

Her legs barely worked. Her guitar slipped from her hands and crashed on the stage as they dragged her through a side exit, past a burning banner where her own face smiled back from the melting promotional art.

The green room door slammed shut behind them with a sound like a coffin closing.

Mark was already there, pacing the small space. He was a caged animal. His face was flushed red with fury, his carefully styled hair disheveled.

"What the FUCK was that? What the actual fuck, Ronnie?" His British accent sharp enough to cut glass.

She opened her mouth to speak, but the words were hard to assemble. "I just ... I wanted—"

"You wanted WHAT? To commit career suicide in front of thirty thousand paying punters?" His voice climbed louder with each word, spittle flying from his lips. "Bloody hell, that's exactly what you did! These people already thought you were fake, and you just proved you haven't got a clue about your own audience!"

The red lip gloss was sticky on her cheek, mixing with her tears. She could taste it, artificial cherry and the salt of her own destruction.

"You think you're some misunderstood artist? Some authentic bloody genius?" Mark's laugh was ugly, vicious. "I've got news for you, love. You're a lip gloss advert with delusions of grandeur! A complete muppet! I turned you, a nobody, into a brand worth millions, and you just torched the lot to sing some pretentious bollocks about posers! The only poser here is you, Riot. A manufactured pop punk Barbie that I sodding well created."

She sank onto the green room's ratty couch, her whole body shaking. The sequined top that had seemed so rebellious an hour ago now felt like a costume. "Mark, pl—"

"Shut it!" he interrupted. "You know what's wrong with you fuckin' Yanks? You're always bloody looking for pain!" He grabbed a bottle from the craft table and hurled it at the wall, water exploding across the room. "Right then, if it's pain you want, I'll give you pain. You're finished. Done. No one in this industry will touch you with a bargepole!"

Mark's gaze landed on the phone, its camera glinting under the room's stark lighting. His expression tightened into fury as he stepped in and swatted at the cameraman.

"YOU! TURN THAT FUCKING PHONE OFF! NOW!"

The camera jerked, the image tilting wildly before steadying again. The sound of the manager's footsteps stomped toward the door, each step like a nail in her professional coffin. The door slammed with violent finality, leaving her completely alone with the aftermath of her choices.

She collapsed forward, her face in her hands, the bright red smear across her cheek catching the green room's harsh fluorescent light.

"Oh my GOD, pause it! Go back to the lip gloss part!"

The airplane cabin came into sharp focus around the phone screen. Two teenage girls hunched over the device in seats 21A and 21B, their faces lit by the glow of viral disaster. One of them jabbed at the screen with a manicured finger, rewinding to the moment of impact.

"That's so brutal," the other girl whispered, loud enough to carry over the engine noise. "Like, you can actually see her soul leaving her body."

Ronnie Mills pressed herself deeper into seat 23D, the baseball cap pulled low over her eyes, oversize sunglasses hiding what she hoped was an unrecognizable face. The whiskey she'd ordered burned in her throat. It was 10 a.m. on a Sunday morning, and she was drinking airplane liquor while teenagers two rows ahead dissected the worst moment of her life like it was entertainment.

"That's totally her, right?" The girl with the phone glanced back over her shoulder. "Same mouth, same nose."

"She looks so different, though. Like, bigger? And her hair."

"It's definitely her. My sister had that red lip gloss. It was like her whole personality for six months."

"Should we ask for a selfie?"

"Ew, no. Ugh, she's just a nobody now."

Ronnie's hand tightened around her whiskey. The flight attendant had given her a look when she'd ordered it, but then, after noticing her despair, passed her a double without charge. Eight years since that night at the Hard Rock. Eight years of running, hiding, and trying to disappear ... safer, smaller, and, frankly, forgettable.

The plane began its descent toward Miami, and she stared out the small window at the bright blue water below. Somewhere down there was the Elysian Serenade, where she'd spend the next week performing safe covers for tourists who had no idea that the quiet blonde woman with the acoustic guitar used to set stages on fire.

She used to be somebody worth destroying.

RIOT AMBER

The Port of Miami buzzed with the choreographed bustle of departure day. Families posed for selfies against the backdrop of massive cruise ships. Couples wore matching vacation T-shirts. Groups clustered around luggage that broadcasted their loyalty to various cruise lines. Ronnie moved through it all like a ghost, practiced in the art of not being noticed.

She found the porters handling musical equipment easily enough. Her gear stood out among the usual suitcases and garment bags: a beat-up Martin acoustic guitar case covered in travel stickers from better times and a basic sound setup that screamed "working musician" rather than "passenger."

"Ronnie Mills," she told the porter, showing him her paperwork. "Musician for Mingle at Sea."

He looked at her gear. She shifted her grip on the guitar case, her thumb instinctively covering the spot where the leather handle had cracked and been wrapped with electrical tape. The small carry-on beside her had a frayed strap she'd meant to replace for months; she angled it away from his line of sight.

"Where's your luggage tags?" he asked.

"Tags?" She squinted. "What tags?"

"You're supposed to have luggage tags, so I know where to send your bags." He let out a huff and turned to grab a pile of unmarked tags. "What's your cabin number?"

She fumbled through her paperwork, pages slipping against each other while a family behind her waited with matched Louis Vuitton luggage. "Here it is ... 4216."

"First cruise?"

"Yeah." She watched him load her guitar case onto a cart, wincing when it got jostled against someone's oversized Rimowa. Hotel bars were predictable. This felt like stepping into unknown territory, trusting her livelihood to processes she didn't understand and people who had no reason to care.

"Oh, hey, dear … you must be Ronnie."

She turned to find a woman advancing like she already knew the ending of the story. Chestnut hair with bold silver streaks was tied back with a scarf that refused to be subtle. Her skin was sun-worn in the way of someone who collects days outside instead of trinkets inside. A soft blue dress floated around her, and her shells-and-silver necklace winked in the light as if it had its own sense of humor.

"I'm Maude, your host coordinator." The woman's voice carried a slight accent Ronnie couldn't place, warm and weathered like driftwood. "Welcome to Mingle at Sea."

Maude handed her a folder containing her performance schedule and a ship map. "Your first performance is tonight at the welcome mixer. Nothing too ambitious. Covers that get people singing along, feeling comfortable."

"That's what I do." The lie came easily after years of practice.

"We're so excited to have you join us for this sailing. You're going to…" She paused. But then Maude studied her with ocean-blue eyes that seemed to see more than Ronnie was comfortable revealing.

"What, do I have something on my face?"

"Oh, no, my dear. I was just saying that I'm really excited to hear your music this week."

"Thanks, but it's not really my songs that I perform; it's just playing a bit of music and blending into the background."

"Nonsense. The heart remembers songs the voice has forgotten."

Before Ronnie could ask what that meant, Maude was already floating away toward another group of passengers. Ronnie stared after her, unsettled by the cryptic comment and the feeling that she'd just been seen through by a complete stranger.

The Elysian Serenade rose from the port with the kind of understated elegance that screamed serious money. Inside, the towering marble atrium stretched three stories above her, its cascading crystal chandelier refracting light throughout the space like scattered diamonds. Ronnie had performed in places like this before, back when she could afford to stay in them rather than work in them. The familiar ache of displacement settled in her chest - luxury venues and first-class treatment, when every door had opened for her, and every expense account had been limitless.

Now she was the hired entertainment, not a paying guest. The difference was subtle but unmistakable in the way people looked past her instead of at her.

Her cabin was small but clean, an interior stateroom on Deck 4 that felt more akin to an oversize walk-in closet. She unpacked quickly, hanging up the few nice outfits she'd brought for performances, arranging her collection of red lipsticks on the tiny vanity like soldiers preparing for battle. Everything else folded neatly into drawers that barely accommodated her week's worth of clothes.

She caught her reflection in the mirror and paused. Natural blonde hair, understated makeup that was miles away from the heavy contouring of her Riot days, except for the red lipstick that had been her favorite shade since middle school. The face looking back at her was older, softer, marked by eight years of hiding from herself.

"Who are you today, Ronnie?" she asked her reflection.

The answer, as always, was whoever she needed to be to get through the next few hours.

The Topaz Lounge sparkled with art deco luxury, chandeliers casting rainbow fragments over jewel-toned velvet. Gold fixtures reflected soft light as about forty guests settled around cocktail tables, the Mingle at Sea group full of first-night anticipation. Her performance space sat in a quiet corner, modest and softly lit.

She settled into her chair, guitar across her lap, adjusting the microphone while pretending to tune already-perfect strings. The room buzzed with lively conversation, drinks flowing as introductions formed. She looked out at the mix of faces, most of them glowing with talk of "finding love at sea" and "new beginnings."

Everyone's running from something, she thought cynically as she watched them mingle.

A woman stepped toward the small stage area. Not flashy or loud, but she commanded a presence that clicked the room into attention. Maude moved with casual authority, holding her glass up and giving the crowd a nod like they were all in on the same joke.

"Good evening, sailors," Maude said, her voice carrying easily over the conversation. "Welcome aboard the Elysian Serenade."

The room quieted, people turning toward her with the respect of passengers who recognized their host.

"You're all here because something called to you," Maude continued, her voice carrying gentle authority like she'd welcomed thousands of travelers. "Maybe it was curiosity. Maybe it was hope. Maybe it was just the need to be somewhere different from where you were yesterday." She gestured toward the windows where the ocean stretched to the horizon. "The beautiful thing about being at sea is that you can't go backward, only forward. So whatever brought you here, let it carry you where you need to go."

A few people nodded, and Maude smiled warmly.

"Don't worry about being perfect. Don't worry about having a plan. Just be present for whatever finds you."

"You don't have to be charming. You don't have to be brave. You just have to show up."

The words hit harder than they should have. Ronnie's fingers found a chord progression automatically, muscle memory keeping her hands busy while her mind processed Maude's simple challenge.

Maude raised her glass higher. "To new beginnings."

"To new beginnings," the room echoed back.

Maude's eyes found Ronnie's across the space, and she gestured toward the performance corner. "Now, let's start this journey with some music. Please welcome Ronnie."

Scattered applause greeted her as she shifted forward in her chair. No fanfare, no introduction beyond her first name. She liked it that way.

"Hi everyone, I'm Ronnie," she said into the microphone, her voice steady and professional. "I'm here to provide some music for your evening."

She launched into "Wonderwall" without further ceremony, her fingers finding the familiar chord progression while her voice wrapped around the melody that everyone knew by heart. Within a few bars, voices joined hers from around the room, creating that warm communal feeling that made cruise performances worthwhile.

"Mr. Brightside" followed, and the energy in the room lifted. She could see faces now, relaxing into the familiar routine of safe covers. An older gentleman nodded along approvingly, while conversations paused between songs as people settled into the music. Her voice warmed up, finding its strength in the comfortable space between performer and audience.

She was starting to relax when a voice called out from the crowd.

"Hey, can you play 'Riot' by Three Days Grace?"

Her fingers froze on the guitar strings, the chord breaking off into an uncomfortable quiet. The word landed with a jarring force, even though she knew immediately it had nothing to do with her. But hearing it here, surrounded by these people, sent panic tightening through her like a familiar old grip.

She forced a smile, professional and deflecting. "Sorry, I don't know that one."

The young man who'd made the request looked genuinely surprised. "Really? It's pretty famous! You know, 'Let's start a riot ... a riot ...'" he started singing the chorus before she cut him off.

"I'm more of a 'songs everyone can sing drunk' kind of guitarist," she said, getting a few chuckles from the crowd. Without missing another beat, she transitioned into "Sweet Caroline," letting the opening notes pull the audience into participation mode.

"Sweet Caroline!" they sang back, and she felt the moment pass.

But even as she played, even as the crowd sang along and the energy lifted, she felt a different kind of attention on her. A man near the back leaned against the bar, silent while the others joined in. He watched her with a curious, measured focus that pressed past the walls she usually kept in place.

She told herself to stop looking. She lasted maybe three heartbeats. His face had that annoying kind of pull, not the "oh my god, it's her" kind, but the "I see you anyway" kind. It felt personal in a way she didn't consent to.

She finished strong with "Since U Been Gone," letting her voice show its range while keeping the song familiar enough for the crowd to stay with her. The applause was genuinely warm, appreciative without being overwhelming.

"Thank you all, enjoy your evening," she said, already reaching for her guitar cable to start packing up.

The crowd began to disperse, conversations resuming as people moved toward other venues or claimed tables for longer conversations. She worked efficiently, wrapping cables and tucking her guitar into its case with practiced speed.

"Your voice has this quality," a voice said beside her, and she looked up to find the man from the back of the room. Up close, he was probably late twenties, with warm brown skin and genuinely kind eyes. "Like you actually lived the songs you're singing."

She went very still, defensive walls slamming into place. "They're just covers."

"I know," he said, and his tone was thoughtful rather than pushy. "That's what makes it interesting."

She didn't know how to respond to that, so she kept packing her equipment, hyperaware of his presence beside her.

"I'm Jerome, by the way."

"Ronnie."

She expected him to push for more conversation, to ask the usual questions about how long she'd been performing or whether she wrote original music. Instead, he just nodded.

"See you around, Ronnie."

He walked off, and she was left with her guitar case and an unwelcome prickle along her spine. It felt as if he had cut through the polished version of herself and caught a glimpse of the part she rarely let surface.

She finished packing in silence, Jerome's words echoing in her mind. *Like you actually lived the songs you're singing.*

If only he knew how hard she'd been working to avoid living anything at all.

Two

The digits on her clock mocked Ronnie from her nightstand, glaring back 11:47 p.m. ...

12:23 a.m. ...

1:15 a.m. ...

She stared at the ceiling of her small interior cabin, listening to the steady hum of the ship's engines and the distant sound of laughter from passengers still enjoying the late-night venues.

Sleep wasn't happening.

Every time she closed her eyes, the voice from the lounge resurfaced. Can you play "Riot" by Three Days Grace? The question had hit harder than it should have, even though she knew instantly it referred to a completely different song. Yet hearing that word in that room had sent panic tightening through her ribs.

She rolled over, pulling the pillow over her head. The ship rocked gently, a motion that should have been soothing but only reminded her that she was trapped on this floating hotel for the next six days.

Six days of performing safe covers for tourists, six days of hoping nobody would make the connection between the quiet blonde woman with the acoustic guitar and the viral disaster from eight years ago.

And then there was Jerome. The way he'd watched her, not singing along like the others. Just observing with those careful, curious eyes that seemed to see more than she was comfortable showing. *Your voice has this quality. Like you actually lived the songs you're singing.*

What did that even mean?

At 2:45 a.m., she gave up. Threw on flip-flops over her bare feet and pulled a light cardigan over her old band t-shirt. The shirt was from some Denver venue where she'd played a weekend gig last month, nothing that would connect to her past. Just Ronnie, the hotel bar performer, trying to make rent.

The late hour left the corridors dim and calm, the emergency lights turning the ship into a muted maze. A few drunk passengers wobbled past her, laughing until their cabin doors swallowed the sound. Night stripped the Elysian Serenade of its showy charm. It became a floating neighborhood of people carrying more baggage than their suitcases could hold.

She found herself on the Lido Deck, drawn by the promise of fresh air and fewer witnesses to her restlessness. The outdoor space was mostly empty except for a few scattered passengers at distant tables, their conversations low and intimate. Stars were visible above the ship's lights, scattered across the dark sky like spilled diamonds.

The twenty-four-hour soft-serve station waited near the pool, an industrial block of metal offering exactly the sort of simple comfort she needed. She moved toward it slowly, eyeing the maze of buttons and levers that appeared more complex than the equipment she had used for her performance.

"Okay," she muttered, pressing what she hoped was the right combination of buttons. "How hard can this be?"

The machine hummed, obedient for once, and vanilla piled into her cup in a smooth, perfect coil. Ronnie held her breath like she was defusing something.

Then the coil sagged. The hum turned into a grind. The machine gave up entirely.

"Shit." She slapped the side of it like that was a thing people did in movies. Nothing. She hit a button. Nothing again. "Of course."

"Here, you have to hit it right," a voice said behind her, and she turned to find Jerome approaching. He looked rumpled in the way people do when they've been trying and failing to sleep, his hair slightly mussed and his hotel-branded polo wrinkled. "There."

He demonstrated with practiced ease, giving the side of the machine a firm smack with his palm. The machine immediately started working again, soft-serve flowing perfectly.

She stared at him. "You have soft-serve expertise?"

He grinned, the expression transforming his tired face. "Insomnia and unlimited soft-serve are a dangerous combination. I may have spent some time figuring out this exact machine at work."

"You look like you've had a rough night too."

"My friend brought someone back to our cabin." He shrugged, settling into a chair at a nearby table. "They're ... ah ... not quiet, if you know what I mean."

Ronnie laughed despite herself. "Ah. Sexiled. A cruise tradition."

"Aaron thinks every port is his personal dating app." Jerome watched her fill her cup with vanilla soft-serve. "I'm discovering there aren't many quiet places to hide on a cruise ship at three in the morning."

She got her ice cream and joined him at his table, settling into the chair across from him. The ocean stretched endlessly around them, dark water meeting darker sky at a horizon she couldn't see.

"Is that what you're doing? Hiding?"

"Aren't we all?" He had gotten his own ice cream and was stirring it absently with a plastic spoon. "What's your excuse for being awake at this hour?"

"Brain won't shut off." She took a bite of ice cream, the cold sweetness exactly what she hadn't known she needed. "Too much thinking."

"About the performance tonight?"

She went still. "Why would you ask that?"

"Because you looked like you were thinking pretty hard when you were packing up your guitar." His voice was gentle, understanding. "My friend Aaron performed in college theater. He'd always replay his shows afterward, wondering if he'd forgotten a line or hit a wrong note."

The explanation eased the tight pull inside her. Just nerves, nothing more. "It went fine. Standard hotel bar set. Play what they want and keep the room steady."

"Is that what you usually do? Hotel bars?"

"Among other things. Weekend gigs, private parties, whatever pays the bills." She found herself settling back in her chair, the defensive tension leaving her shoulders. "You said you work in hotels?"

"Hotel management. Colorado Springs." He grinned. "So I've seen plenty of lobby performers over the years. Good ones and terrible ones."

"Which category do I fall into?"

"Definitely the good category. Actually, better than most I've heard. You can tell you actually care about music, not just going through the motions."

She studied his face, looking for hidden meaning, but found only genuine appreciation. "What kind of hotel?"

"Business travelers mostly. Convention center attached, lots of conferences and corporate events." He seemed to relax as they moved to safer topics. "You'd be amazed at how demanding people can be about the free breakfast buffet."

"Oh, I believe it. I work hotel bar shifts sometimes. People treat you like you're personally responsible for every inconvenience in their lives."

"Exactly!" His eyes lit up with shared understanding. "Like the time this guest insisted I personally find her lost earring. Not hotel security, not housekeeping. Me. The manager. At two in the morning."

"Did you find it?"

"In the parking lot, somehow. Never did figure out how it got there."

They traded hospitality horror stories as the night deepened around them. Ronnie found herself laughing more than she had in months, sharing her own tales of drunk customers and impossible requests. Jerome had a gift for storytelling, turning mundane hotel disasters into comedy gold.

"The worst was this corporate group," she said, gesturing with her spoon. "They booked me for what they said was a 'quiet dinner party.' Turns out it was their annual sales meeting, and they expected me to provide background music while their CEO screamed at everyone about quarterly projections."

"How long did you last?"

"Two songs. Then I packed up and told them they could keep my deposit if it meant I could keep my sanity."

"Good for you. Some audiences aren't worth the paycheck."

There was a note in his tone that hinted he had learned that lesson the hard way. She found herself imagining the situations he must have handled in hotel management, the kind that left a person calm only because they had survived worse.

Without realizing it, they had settled in more comfortably during their conversation. Empty ice cream cups pushed aside as they leaned forward, engaged in easy conversation that flowed from work stories to travel observations to childhood memories.

"So you grew up in Denver?" he asked.

"Born and raised. You?"

"Vegas, actually. Very different childhood than most people, I imagine."

"Let me guess. Your parents weren't showgirls and dealers?"

He laughed. "Insurance agents. Both of them. They met at an actuarial conference."

"That might be the most unromantic meet-cute story I've ever heard."

"They used to joke that they checked the odds and agreed they were a smart bet." His grin softened. "Thirty-five years in, I think they proved themselves right."

"That's really sweet."

"They hoped I'd join them in insurance, but I took security jobs at UNLV. Long nights at concerts and conventions. I ended up loving how hotels worked behind the scenes. The management part felt like puzzle solving, and I wanted more of that."

Their conversation drifted into family with a quiet honesty that moved walls aside gently. He described parents who modeled steady love. She confessed that her sister's kids adored her, guest room and all. Childhood plans floated to the surface, altered by the unpredictable turns that carve life into shapes both rougher and, at times, unexpectedly better.

"Did you always want to work in music?" he asked.

"I wanted to be a rock star when I was sixteen. Didn't we all?" She kept her tone light, truthful but vague.

"What changed your mind?"

"Oh, you know. Life." She shrugged, keeping her tone light. "Reality has a way of adjusting expectations."

He nodded as he understood completely. "That's why I chose hotel management over event planning. I thought I wanted to create big experiences for people, but it turns out I prefer taking care of them in smaller ways. Making sure their room is ready, their needs are met, their problems are solved."

"You're really good at storytelling," she said, still laughing from his latest hotel disaster tale.

"Years of practice. You learn to find the humor in chaos when you work in hospitality."

"I could say the same about you. Most hotel bar performers are just marking time until their real gig comes along. You actually care about the music."

"Even when it's just covers?"

"Especially then. It takes real skill to make another artist's song feel like it belongs to you."

The observation hit deeper than it should have. For eight years she'd worn other people's songs like armor, familiar chords and safe lyrics between her and the world. Jerome didn't call it hiding. He called it art. And that shift landed like a hand at the small of her back.

Ronnie didn't trust herself to speak. She stared out at the dark water until her heartbeat stopped trying to sprint. Jerome's presence stayed steady beside her, not demanding anything, not pulling. People drifted past and away again, and somehow the two of them remained, a small pocket of stillness the rest of the ship didn't seem to notice.

"Can I ask you something?" she said.

"Sure."

"Are you enjoying this cruise so far? The whole singles thing?"

He considered the question. "Aaron is convinced this trip will change my life. Find me the perfect woman, cure my chronic bachelorhood, solve all my problems with vitamin sea therapy."

"Vitamin sea?"

"His term, not mine. He has theories about ocean air and romance."

"And you don't believe in his theories?"

"I think Aaron watches too many romantic comedies." Jerome's smile was fond despite his words. "But he's a good friend. And I needed to get away from work for a while, so here I am."

"Here you are, talking to the cruise entertainment at three in the morning instead of mingling with eligible singles."

"Are you complaining?"

Ronnie opened her mouth, then closed it again. She'd been so busy existing in the moment she hadn't done her usual thing. No complaining. No deflection. No turning it into a bit.

This was what it felt like to be seen as Ronnie, not Riot. To be listened to without being sized up. Her throat tightened with the strange ache of it, like her body remembered what normal used to feel like.

"No," she said quietly. "I'm not complaining."

The eastern horizon was beginning to lighten, she realized with surprise. Not full dawn yet, but that subtle shift from black sky to deep blue that promised sunrise was coming.

"Oh my God, what time is it?" she asked, looking around as if the time might be written in the stars.

Jerome checked his phone. "Six a.m."

"Six?" She stared at him in disbelief. "We've been talking for three hours?"

"Apparently so."

They both relaxed into their chairs, taking a breath as the truth of it settled. Three hours had slipped by with the ease of half an hour. A rare conversation had unfolded, one that dissolved time and left the rest of the world on mute.

"I haven't stayed up all night just talking to someone in…" She paused, trying to remember, "God, I can't remember how long."

"Me neither. This is either the best or worst cruise decision I've made so far."

"Why would it be the worst?"

"Because now I'm going to be completely useless today. But I regret nothing."

His grin was contagious. She smiled back, feeling lighter than she had in months. When was the last time she had enjoyed another person's company this much? When was the last time she had felt like herself instead of a carefully constructed version meant to dodge recognition or trouble?

"I should probably try to get some sleep before I have to be functional," she said, though she made no move to leave.

"Same. Though I'm not sure sleep is happening at this point."

"Are you planning to do any of the morning Mingle activities? I think there's a cooking class at 9:30."

"Not really my thing. I'm supposed to stay available in case they need music for anything, but I mostly avoid the group stuff."

"Aaron will probably drag me to something. He's very committed to the 'full cruise experience.'"

They both stood up, gathering their things with the reluctance of people who didn't want a perfect moment to end. The walk back into the ship felt natural, their conversation continuing as they made their way through corridors that were still quiet but already showing signs of early-morning activity.

The elevator started down, and the quiet between them felt chosen, not awkward. Ronnie watched Jerome in the soft light, the way he didn't try to perform being okay. He just was. Even exhausted, he carried himself with a kind of ease that made her chest feel oddly tight.

"Thanks for a pleasant date," she said suddenly, the words slipping out before she could think better of them.

Jerome's eyebrows shot up. "Is that what this was?" His smile shifted softer, more curious. "I hope so."

"I don't know, but it was nicer than most first dates I've had." She felt her cheeks warm. "I mean, if it was a date. Which it probably wasn't. I just meant—"

"It was definitely better than most first dates," he said quickly, saving her from further rambling. "Even if we never figured out if that's what we're calling it."

The elevator dinged softly as they reached his floor. The doors opened, but Jerome didn't immediately step out. They both hesitated, neither quite ready for the moment to end.

"So," she said.

"So," he repeated, grinning.

"You should probably get some sleep."

"Probably." He stepped out but turned back to face her, holding the elevator doors open with one hand. "See you around, Ronnie."

"See you around, Jerome."

The doors slid closed, stealing him away with a final glimpse of his smile.

Ronnie steadied herself in the hallway and headed for her cabin, tired in the limbs but awake in the soul.

Back in her small interior cabin, she kicked off her flip-flops and fell onto the bed, still wearing her cardigan and band t-shirt. Through the thin walls, she could hear the gentle sounds of the ship waking up around her, but for the first time in hours, her restless mind had finally quieted.

The digital clock on her nightstand blinked 8:32 a.m. as the numbers blurred and her eyes slipped closed.

Three

The soft white sand felt like powdered sugar between Ronnie's toes as she settled into her carefully chosen spot on the beach. She'd positioned herself among the other passengers scattered across the beautiful stretch of sand, close enough to the massive Margaritaville pool complex to blend in but far enough away to maintain the illusion of anonymity.

Her oversized sunglasses and wide-brimmed hat created a protective barrier as she opened her paperback romance, some mindless escapist fiction she'd grabbed from the ship's library.

The crystal-clear Caribbean water stretched endlessly, and the familiar sounds of vacation surrounded her: children laughing in the pool, the distant whir of the FlowRider, conversations in multiple languages drifting on the warm breeze.

This was perfect. She could hear the Mingle group's laughter from their rented cabana somewhere behind her, but she felt safely invisible among the dozens of other cruise passengers claiming their own patches of paradise.

Yesterday had been spent hiding in her cabin, listening to the sounds of group activities through the ship's corridors. The cooking class, the trivia contests, and the organized fun she couldn't bring herself to join. She'd ordered room service and practiced guitar alone, replaying her 3 a.m. conversation with Jerome until she'd almost convinced herself she'd imagined the connection entirely.

Out here, where tourists drifted in bright clusters and the day moved at beach speed, she could finally breathe. The one-piece kept most of her ink under wraps, except the cherry bomb on her right shoulder. At her hip, the suit's hem still surrendered a glimpse of her waist tattoo, platform heels and fishnet legs. She tucked her natural blonde hair under the hat, lowered the brim, and stepped into the simplest disguise she'd ever wanted. A stranger.

"Mind if I steal a moment of your beautiful morning?"

Ronnie looked up to find Maude approaching, her flowing sea-blue caftan moving gracefully between beach chairs and other passengers. The Mingle host settled beside her in the sand without waiting for permission, though her manner was warm rather than intrusive.

"Maude." Ronnie closed her book, resigned. "How did you find me?"

"You're not hiding, dear. You're just blending." Maude's smile was knowing but kind. "There's a difference."

"I'm taking a quiet day. Nothing wrong with that, right?"

"Nothing at all." Maude gazed out at the water, her voice carrying that gentle authority Ronnie remembered from the welcome mixer. "But you're part of the Mingle family this week, Ronnie. Families don't avoid each other."

"I'm not avoiding anyone. I'm just …" Ronnie gestured toward the other beachgoers around them. "Enjoying the beach like everyone else."

"Sometimes the songs we're meant to hear only play when we're brave enough to join the orchestra."

Despite herself, Ronnie almost smiled. "Is that another one of your ocean metaphors?"

"Music metaphor this time. I try to vary them." Maude's eyes twinkled with humor. "The group rented a cabana right over there. There is laughter, good company, and a man who keeps checking the beach for a certain musician."

Ronnie's pulse quickened despite her best efforts. "Who?"

"The ocean always knows when to retreat, dear. Trust yourself to know too." Maude stood, brushing sand from her caftan. "Even the tide returns after retreating. Don't be afraid to come back in."

The mention of someone looking for her had created an unwanted flutter of curiosity. Ronnie realized her "hiding in plain sight" strategy had been completely transparent to Maude, which was both annoying and oddly comforting.

"Just for an hour," she heard herself say.

The transition from anonymous beachgoer to group member took only a few steps, but it felt like crossing into another world. The cabana buzzed with conversation and laughter, tropical drinks appearing and disappearing as people settled into vacation mode. Steel drums drifted from the bar area, mixing with the splash of pool games and the easy chatter of people who'd decided to like each other for a week.

About fifteen members of the Mingle group were scattered between the shaded cabana seating and the pool itself. The natural division was obvious: pool people radiating energetic vacation vibes, cabana people preferring conversation and shade.

Ronnie immediately gravitated toward the cabana.

"Ronnie!" The warm calls came from people she remembered from the welcome mixer. A woman stepped forward and placed a tropical drink in her hand before she had the chance to settle in, the sort of effortless kindness that cruises seemed to invite.

Jerome was in the pool with Aaron, who talked with full-arm enthusiasm while Jerome followed along with patient interest. When Jerome looked toward the cabana, recognition flickered across his face, followed by relief. Their eyes held for a moment before Aaron pulled him back in, and the brief exchange left her steadier than she expected.

"Well, look who decided to join the party," Tony said, patting the cushioned seat beside him. The seventy-year-old widower had a Corona in one hand and a contented smile as he watched the pool activity. "I was hoping you'd show up."

"Maude can be very persuasive."

"That she can." Tony's laugh was warm. "But I'm glad she convinced you. That was lovely the other night, dear. Really lovely."

"Thank you." Ronnie settled into the comfortable seating, surprised by how natural it felt.

"Made me think of my Marie. She always said music shows who people really are."

Tony had a way about him that encouraged honesty. It might have been the gentle way he spoke of his late wife or the open appreciation he offered without any strings attached. Whatever created that calm, it nudged her shoulders down and let her breathe easier.

"You know," Tony continued, taking a sip of his beer, "I taught high school music for forty years. Heard a lot of kids sing."

"Oh, really? That must have been rewarding."

"Best job in the world. I only complained when we hit the budget meetings." He laughed. "And you, you lead with heart. No one can train a person to do that."

They fell into that familiar, back-and-forth flow. Tony talked about his classroom days, about meeting Marie as a school dance chaperone, about retirement and the strange quiet it left behind. Ronnie surprised herself by leaning in, asking questions without turning each one into a test.

Jerome had made his way to their side of the pool and rested at the edge, close enough to catch their conversation. Sunlight glinted off the droplets on his shoulders as he laughed at Aaron's comment, and Ronnie's attention drifted from Tony's story about the jazz band to the effortless way Jerome moved, each motion smooth and unhurried.

"Earth to Ronnie," Tony said with gentle amusement. "I was telling you about the time our bass player showed up to prom in flip-flops."

"Sorry." Heat crept up her neck. "I was just ..."

"Admiring the view?" Tony's eyes twinkled with knowing humor. "Nothing wrong with that, dear. Marie used to say the heart notices what the mind hasn't figured out yet." When their eyes met again, she felt that same flutter from their late-night 3 a.m. ice cream talks.

"You know who would have loved hearing you sing?" Tony said, settling back in his chair with the easy satisfaction of a man who had all day and nowhere to be. "My granddaughter Sophia."

"Tell me about her."

"That girl went through quite the phase in middle school. All angry music and attitude." His fond smile suggested he'd enjoyed every minute of it. "Posters covering every inch of her walls, music blasting until her parents thought the house might shake apart."

"Teenage rebellion?"

"Oh, more than that. She was working through some things, you know? Her parents were beside themselves, but I told them to let her feel what she needed to feel."

Tony's affection was contagious. Ronnie was asking about his granddaughter before she could stop herself.

"What kind of music?"

"Loud. Raw. The kind that makes parents worry but sometimes helps kids survive." He took another sip of his beer. "Spent every penny of her allowance on this bright red lip gloss. Some flavor with a silly name."

Ronnie went very still. Her fingers tightened around her drink.

"From some singer she was crazy about." Tony continued, completely oblivious to the way the blood had drained from Ronnie's face. "Sophia would wear that lip gloss every single day. Said it made her feel brave."

The tropical drink in Ronnie's hand suddenly felt too heavy. Cherry Bomb. It had to be Cherry Bomb lip gloss that had made his granddaughter feel brave.

"A bright red lip gloss," she managed, her voice carefully controlled.

"That's right. She'd put it on like war paint before school every morning." Tony's expression grew more thoughtful. "You know what

I loved about that whole phase? She stopped being afraid to be herself."

Ronnie nodded, not trusting her voice.

From the pool, Jerome picked up on the shift. His focus slipped away from Aaron and landed on her, even though he tried to mask it. Their eyes met across the space, and she managed a smile that felt too tight to hold.

"Even after that singer had her hard moment online," Tony continued, tone soft but firm. "It went viral. People piled on. Sophia still defended her. She looked at me and said, 'Grandpa, she was just telling the truth.'"

The words landed with unwelcome force. Ronnie nodded again and reached for her drink, hoping the slight tremor in her fingers stayed hidden. Under the table, her other hand dug into the fabric of her cover-up at her thigh.

Tony was completely unaware of the earthquake he'd just triggered. "Sophia's in college now, studying social work. Still has that fire in her, just channeled differently. She calls me every Sunday, always asks if I'm 'staying young.' That's her phrase."

"She sounds wonderful."

"You remind me of her a little. Same age, same ..." He paused, searching for the word. "Spirit, maybe."

"Same age?" Ronnie's eyebrows shot up, and she couldn't help but laugh. "Tony, how old do you think I am?"

"Oh, twenty-two, twenty-three? Same as Sophia."

"Twenty-two?" Ronnie nearly choked on her drink, delighted. "Oh my God, Tony, you just made my entire week. I'm thirty-five."

Tony gaped. "Thirty-five? No way."

"Way." Ronnie smiled, bright and unguarded. "And please keep going. I've earned this."

"Well, I'll be damned." Tony shook his head, studying her face with new appreciation. "Marie always said I was terrible at guessing ages, but thirty-five? You've got that young energy about you. Whatever you're doing, keep doing it."

Ronnie asked about Sophia's studies, needing to anchor herself in the moment. Tony's stories about his granddaughter's volunteer work and her commitment to helping teenagers created the image of a young woman who had grown into a steady and compassionate person.

"She always says she learned about standing up for people from that music phase."

The conversation continued, Tony sharing more about Sophia's college life while Ronnie processed the devastating beauty of his innocent love for his granddaughter. Every fond memory he shared hit her differently now that she understood the connection. This wasn't just any teenager who'd been helped by her music. This was Tony's granddaughter, this sweet man who was sitting beside her, talking about his Sophia with such obvious pride and affection.

Her attention slid back to the pool, where Jerome floated on his back with his eyes closed and his arms loose at his sides. The calm on his face, the quiet trust it took to let the water hold him, sent a tight pull through her that had nothing to do with Tony's news.

"You know," Tony said, following her gaze with a small smile, "I've been watching young people fall in love for forty years. The signs are always the same."

Ronnie's attention snapped back to him. "I'm not—"

"Course not," he said easily, taking another sip of his Corona. "Just making an observation."

"You know what I told Sophia when her parents wanted her to take down those posters?" Tony said.

"What?"

"I said, 'Let her keep what makes her feel strong. Life will take enough away as it is.'" He looked directly at Ronnie. "Sometimes the things that help us survive don't look pretty to other people."

Tony had no idea he was talking to the woman whose poster had covered his granddaughter's walls, whose lip gloss had made Sophia feel brave, whose viral meltdown Sophia had defended with the fierce loyalty of a teenager who felt understood.

Ronnie eased into the cabana cushions as the truth settled over her. She had spent eight years convinced she had let her fans down and tarnished what they once cherished. Yet Tony's memories painted another picture. The Cherry Bomb lip gloss tied to her most public mistake had given a hurting teenager a sense of courage each day.

Jerome pulled himself out of the pool and took his towel, drops sliding from his shoulders as he made his way to their cabana. Aaron called to him about heading back, yet Jerome moved at an unhurried pace.

"Good to see you made it out today," he said to Ronnie, his voice carrying warmth that had nothing to do with the Caribbean sun.

Of course, he found her at the moment she was trying not to unravel. Of course, his presence steadied her.

"Maude can be very persuasive."

Their first spoken words of the day arrived layered with the awareness that had grown between every poolside glance. Tony witnessed the moment with a gentle, knowing smile, shaped by decades spent watching young people find their way toward each other.

"You know what I learned from forty years of teaching music?" Tony said quietly.

"What?" Ronnie asked, though part of her attention was still on Jerome's presence.

"Sometimes the songs that scare us the most are the ones we need to sing." He looked at her with those kind eyes that had seen so much. "The brave ones find their voice eventually."

The Caribbean sun blazed overhead, and around them, other Mingle group members were starting to gather their things as someone mentioned needing to head back to the ship soon.

Ronnie watched Jerome help Tony gather his things, the easy kindness in the gesture. Eight years ago, she'd convinced herself that destroying everything was the only honest choice. But maybe Tony was right. Maybe some things deserved to survive, even the messy, complicated, imperfect things.

Maybe especially those.

Four

The next day, the air-conditioned tour bus wound through the Dominican countryside, past sugar cane fields and small villages painted in sun-faded pastels. Ronnie pressed her forehead against the cool window glass, watching palm trees blur by as the morning heat shimmered off the pavement.

"Did you see Tony yesterday at the beach?" Ashley asked from the seat beside her. "He was giving that young couple marriage advice for like an hour. They were hanging on every word like he was some kind of love guru."

"Mm-hmm." Ronnie made an appropriate sound of agreement, though she'd missed whatever Tony had done. Her attention kept drifting forward to where Jerome sat with Aaron three rows ahead.

She studied the back of his head, the light catching in his hair as it slipped through the tinted windows. The bend in the road revealed his profile, focused on the scenery rolling by. He appeared untouched by Aaron's lively retelling of a late-night run-in with a girl and far too much tequila.

"Earth to Ronnie." Ashley nudged her with an elbow. "You okay? You seem distracted."

"Just taking in the views."

Ashley followed the direction of her focus, and Ronnie saw the exact moment understanding dawned on the other woman's face. That knowing smile that meant romance was about to become a topic of conversation.

"He's been looking back here too, you know."

Heat crept up Ronnie's neck. "Who has?"

"Oh, please." Ashley's grin widened. "Jerome. He's turned around at least three times since we left the port."

As if summoned by his name, Jerome glanced back. Their eyes met for a suspended moment before they both looked away, him toward the window, her toward her hands folded in her lap. The eye contact lasted two seconds, but left her pulse stuttering.

"There's nothing ..." Ronnie started.

"Sure, there isn't." Ashley's tone was teasing but kind. "That's why you both look like teenagers caught passing notes in class."

The guide's voice crackled through the bus's speakers. "We're approaching Puerto Plata now! Our first stop will be the famous Amber Museum, where you'll see one of the world's finest collections of Dominican amber. After that, we'll head to a beautiful local beach for swimming and lunch."

"Amber museum? Rocks in a glass case?" Aaron's voice boomed from up front, followed by his signature too-loud laugh. "Wake me when we get to the beach."

Jerome replied, but his voice was too low for Ronnie to catch. She watched him shift slightly away from his friend, a small adjustment Aaron did not seem to notice.

As the bus wound through narrow streets, it passed Victorian-era buildings in worn yellows and blues, the gingerbread trim glowing in the early light. Puerto Plata felt unlike their earlier stops, marked by an older rhythm and a depth that showed through the parts shaped for tourists.

When they finally pulled up to a cheerful yellow mansion with ornate white trim, the guide announced their arrival. "The Museo del Ámbar Dominicano, housed in a villa built by a German immigrant who fell in love here over a hundred years ago."

The bus shifted into a flurry of motion as tourists reached for their bags, checked their cameras, and hurried to apply sunscreen. When Ronnie stood, she was swept into the crush of people funneling toward the one door.

By the time she made it off the bus, the group had naturally started clustering around their guide, a local woman whose voice carried the musical cadence of the islands. Ronnie hovered near the outer edge of the circle, half listening to the introduction about fossilized tree resin millions of years old.

Ashley had already been claimed by another single woman from their group, the two of them comparing notes about their failed attempts at paddleboarding yesterday. Aaron was inserting himself into a cluster of younger women, his voice carrying as he made some joke about finding them all jewelry.

"Gotta spread the Aaron charm equally, bro!" he called back to Jerome, who stood alone near a flowering bougainvillea, looking vaguely uncomfortable with his abandonment.

Ronnie watched Jerome scan the group. When their eyes met again, he didn't look away this time. Instead, he walked over with a slight smile that made her stomach flip.

"Want to be museum buddies?" He gestured toward the mansion's entrance, where people were already starting to file through. "I have a feeling Aaron's going to spend the whole time hitting on that group from New Jersey."

She hesitated just long enough to maintain the illusion that she hadn't been hoping for exactly this. "Sure. Someone needs to make sure you don't break anything priceless."

His smile widened at her small joke. "I make no promises. I'm a hazard in enclosed spaces."

They fell into step together as the group moved into the museum. The temperature dropped immediately inside the old villa, the thick walls holding the Caribbean heat at bay. Dark wood floors creaked beneath their feet, and the air smelled faintly of polish and age.

The first room held a wall of newspaper clippings and movie memorabilia. Ronnie stopped in front of a replica of a walking cane with a fossilized mosquito trapped at its top.

"Jurassic Park," Jerome said, stepping up beside her. "They filmed the opening scene here. Well, not here exactly, but in amber mines nearby."

"You know your dinosaur movie trivia."

"I was eight when I first saw it. Pretty sure I watched it 40 times that summer." He leaned closer to examine the replica. "They found a mosquito in Dominican amber and used it as the premise for the whole franchise. DNA preserved for millions of years."

Ronnie paused over the tiny insect trapped in the amber. The image stirred a tight pull inside her. She stepped to the next display, a spread of pieces sorted by hue. Many held the familiar honey-gold glow, while others shifted into deeper cognac tones and rich reddish browns.

Jerome followed, giving her space while staying close enough for conversation. "This is actually kind of amazing. Look at this one."

He pointed to a piece containing what looked like a perfectly preserved flower, its petals still delicate despite being millions of years old.

"It's strange," Ronnie said quietly, still studying the trapped flower. "Frozen forever in a single moment."

Jerome turned toward her, but she kept her gaze on the display case.

"You say it like you're talking about yourself," he said, gentle, curious without pushing.

She blinked. "What?"

"Like that idea used to make sense to you."

She hadn't realized she'd spoken the thought aloud. Her fingers pressed against the glass, leaving faint prints.

"I used to think I was like that wild ocean we saw from the ship. Untamed. Crashing into things."

"And now?"

"Now I know that being wild just means you break things. Including yourself."

They stood in the museum's chill, boxed in by glass and history. The exhibits had outlived civilizations, and suddenly that felt less like trivia and more like a warning. Tourists passed, close enough to brush shoulders, but their voices landed far away.

"Maybe you just hadn't found the right shore," Jerome said finally.

She turned to look at him then, surprised by the poetry of it. He wasn't looking at the displays anymore, just at her, with an expression that made her chest constrict.

"I used to want to create huge events," he said, turning back to the glass cases. "Music festivals are experiences that would change people's lives. Now I manage a hotel. Same breakfast buffet every single day."

"Why the switch?"

"Sometimes I wonder if I chose predictable because I was scared of failing."

The guide's voice floated in from the next room, calling them toward what she promised was the museum's most spectacular display. They followed, entering a circular chamber where the centerpiece made Ronnie stop mid-step.

The specimens were displayed under special lighting that made them glow with an otherworldly luminescence. What appeared golden-brown in normal light transformed into an ethereal blue under ultraviolet.

"Blue amber," the guide announced. "The rarest variety in the world. It only reveals its true color under certain light."

Jerome looked over and caught her staring. Ronnie didn't flinch away. She let him have the moment.

He nodded toward a larger piece. "That one has a gecko inside. Twenty million years and you can still see every scale."

Ronnie leaned in until the glass edge of the case blurred. The lizard was frozen mid-step, toes splayed, body caught in the most unremarkable motion. A life interrupted so cleanly it felt like a sentence cut off halfway through.

"Do you think it knew?" she asked quietly. "That everything was about to change?"

"I think it was just living its life. And then it got interrupted."

Their shoulders were almost touching now. She could smell his cologne mixed with the faint tropical scent that clung to everyone in this climate. Her breath felt shallow.

"Come on," Jerome said eventually. "I think there's more in the next room."

The rest of the museum tour passed quickly. They moved through rooms filled with insects frozen mid-flight, prehistoric spiders, and plant matter that hadn't existed for millennia. Jerome stayed close, his presence both comfortable and electric.

In the gift shop, he paused at a display of jewelry. He picked up a small pendant, a teardrop of deep golden resin on a simple silver chain, and held it up to the light.

"It's beautiful," Ronnie said.

He set it back down carefully. "We should probably catch the bus. Beach time."

The ride to the beach was short, maybe fifteen minutes.

"Thanks for the museum company," he said quietly. "That was actually really interesting."

"You sound surprised."

"Aaron had me convinced it would be forty-five minutes of looking at rocks." He smiled. "I should trust my own instincts more."

The bus turned a final corner, and a small crescent beach appeared below. La Playita, the guide called it. A hidden gem away from the tourist crowds, soft golden sand meeting impossibly turquoise water.

"Now that's more like it," Jerome said.

They found a spot for their things near some smaller boulders that provided a bit of shade. Ronnie pulled off her cover-up, hyperaware of her one-piece swimsuit and the way it didn't quite hide the tattoo on her hip. The pinup's legs were clearly visible below the suit's edge, fishnets and platform heels that no amount of strategic positioning could conceal.

If Jerome noticed, he let her keep her dignity. Shirt off, no fuss, like he was born on a beach and issued confidence at the door. Ronnie did not stare. She simply looked in his general direction with scientific curiosity.

The water was a small miracle. Warm, clear, gentle, the kind that makes you forget you were tense in the first place. They waded in, sand shifting underfoot. At waist depth, Ronnie dove forward and let the ocean do what oceans do best. Shut her brain up.

When she surfaced, Jerome was treading water nearby, watching her with an expression she couldn't quite read.

"So what would you do," she asked, "if you weren't playing it safe?"

He paused, thinking it over. A playful look followed. "Maybe this."

The splash caught her completely off guard, a wall of water that left her sputtering and laughing.

"Oh, you're going to regret that."

What followed was a carefree water fight that would have made most adults blush, yet neither cared. They splashed and chased each other through the shallows, laughter rising into the quiet stretch of beach. A couple of nearby tourists watched with warm amusement.

When they finally called a truce, they were both breathing hard, standing chest-deep in the crystal water. A strand of Ronnie's hair was plastered across her face, and Jerome reached out to brush it away. His fingers lingered against her cheek.

"There's a place over there," he said, not moving his hand an inch. They stood close enough that she could see the water beading on his eyelashes and feel the warmth rolling from his skin even in the cool water. "Between those rocks. Looks like a small cove."

"Worth exploring?" The word came out breathless.

"I think so." His eyes dropped to her lips for just a moment before meeting hers again. "Want to see?"

Neither of them moved for another heartbeat. Then Jerome stepped back, breaking whatever had been building between them. "Come on. Before someone else discovers it."

She followed him toward the limestone formations at the far end of the beach. The rocks here were soft and sculptured, worn into strange shapes by centuries of patient water.

"There's a gap," Jerome said, pointing to a narrow passage between two large formations. "I think it opens up on the other side."

They waded through knee-deep water, the passage walls rising around them until they blocked out the main beach entirely. Ronnie's hand found the smooth stone for balance, and then they emerged into a space that made her forget to breathe.

A hidden pool, maybe twenty feet across, sheltered on all sides by curving limestone that glowed almost golden in the afternoon light. The water here was utterly still, reflecting the sky like a mirror. Flowering vines had cascaded down one of the rock faces, adding splashes of pink and red to the pale stone.

They were completely alone.

"This can't be real," Ronnie whispered, turning in a slow circle to take it all in.

"I know." Jerome's voice was closer than she expected. She turned to find him watching her with an expression that made her stomach flip. Water droplets still clung to his shoulders, and his hair was pushed back from his face in wet spikes.

They stood there, just looking at each other. Ronnie became hyperaware of everything: the gentle lap of water against stone, the way the filtered sunlight caught the gold flecks in his brown eyes, the rhythm of her own pulse in her ears.

"Ronnie." Just her name, but the way he said it made her take a step closer without thinking.

"Yeah?"

"I really want to kiss you right now."

The honesty of it, the simple declaration without games or pretense, undid her completely. "Oh, thank God," she breathed, and closed the remaining distance between them.

His hands found her waist under the water, steadying them both as she reached up to thread her fingers through his wet hair. They were both trembling slightly, from cold or nerves or want, she couldn't tell. Their lips met tentatively at first, a soft press that tasted of salt water and possibility.

A small sound escaped her, and Jerome tightened his hold. The tentative beginning dropped away, replaced by a connection that surged forward without hesitation.

The kiss deepened, a question transforming into an answer. When she responded by threading her fingers through his hair and pulling him closer, nine years of safe choices melted away. She kissed him with a kind of desperate passion she'd forgotten she was capable of feeling.

The water lapped around them as he pressed her back against the smooth limestone wall. She could taste salt on his lips, feel the sun-warmed stone against her back, the cool water at her waist. Everything was sensation and want and the perfect rightness of this moment that existed outside of real life.

When they broke apart, both breathing raggedly, their foreheads touched.

"We should probably ..." she started.

"Not yet. Please."

The second kiss lingered, slow and intense. His hands worked through her wet hair while she traced the strong lines of his back, learning his body one touch at a time. Everything else fell away until only the cove remained, the water around them, and the man who made *wanting* feel real again.

Eventually, reality intruded in the form of the guide's distant voice calling the group back to the bus. They pulled apart, both trying to calm their breathing.

"We should head back," Jerome said reluctantly.

They squeezed back through the narrow passage and emerged onto the main beach looking thoroughly disheveled. Ronnie was sure everyone could tell exactly what they'd been doing, from their swollen lips to the way they carefully weren't touching.

Aaron's voice cut through the ambient noise immediately. "Where'd you two disappear to?"

"Just exploring," they said simultaneously, which only made it worse.

The group gathered their things and made their way back to the bus. The guide had arranged for a local lunch at a beachside restaurant, rum punch included, and the mood was festive as everyone settled in with their food.

Ronnie tried to create distance, sitting with Tony and another Mingle member, but the group dynamics kept pushing her and Jerome into proximity. Every accidental touch sent electricity through her. When their knees bumped under the table, she nearly knocked over her water glass, reaching to steady herself.

"You two find the best spots?" Tony asked with a wide-eyed curiosity that showed he had no clue what his question implied.

"The cove was beautiful," Ronnie managed, her voice only slightly higher than normal.

She watched Aaron pull Jerome aside toward the bar, probably for another round of rum punch. She could only catch fragments of the conversation, but Aaron's laugh carried. That particular male laugh that meant conquests were being discussed. The rice and beans on her plate suddenly looked unappetizing.

The bus ride back to Amber Cove started with her still floating on the high of that kiss. She deliberately sat with Tony this time, letting him tell her stories about his late wife while she replayed every moment in the hidden pool. Jerome was several rows ahead with Aaron and some other guys from the cruise. Everyone was tired and satisfied, the bus filled with the comfortable chatter of people who'd shared an adventure.

She was watching the countryside roll by, lost in the memory of Jerome's hands in her hair, when Aaron's voice cut through her reverie.

"My boy Jerome finally got some action!"

Her hand froze mid-motion where she'd been tucking hair behind her ear. She kept her eyes on the window, but her attention was laser-focused on the conversation ahead.

"The cruise singer, right?" one of the other guys asked.

"Yeah, she's hot, I'll give him that."

Laughter from the group. Male laughter. The kind that made her skin prickle.

"Just be careful, bro," Aaron continued, his voice carrying easily through the bus. A few rum punches had stripped away any volume control. "Those performer types, they do this every cruise, you know."

"She's probably got a guy in every port," another voice added.

More laughter.

"Part of the entertainment package," someone said.

"Free samples, but you can't take them home," Aaron added, and the group roared.

"Aaron, come on. That's not what this is." Jerome's voice carried for the first time, sharp with irritation.

"What happens at sea stays at sea, right?" Aaron continued, either not hearing or not caring about Jerome's protests.

"Don't catch feelings for the hired help."

Ronnie's fingernails dug into her palms. Every word landed precisely where it would do the most damage. She'd heard Jerome try to defend her, but then his voice dropped again, too quiet to carry. She could see him shaking his head, but was that frustration with Aaron or embarrassment about being called out?

"Come on, you know I'm right," Aaron said loudly.

Jerome said something she couldn't make out.

"It was fun though, right? That's all that matters."

Jerome's silence stretched. And stretched. And stretched.

Ronnie stared at the blur of palm trees and sugar cane through the window, but she wasn't seeing any of it. She was back in a different tour bus, a different lifetime, hearing different men discuss what she was worth. Entertainment value. Merchandise potential. Brand synergy.

Product to be consumed and discarded.

"You okay, dear?" Tony asked, and she realized her jaw was clenched so tight her teeth ached.

"Just tired from all the swimming."

The bus pulled into Amber Cove's cruise terminal. She saw Jerome trying to catch her eye as everyone disembarked, but she kept her focus firmly forward, following Tony toward the ship. Her legs moved automatically, carrying her across the pavement while her mind stayed frozen in that moment of silence.

"That was special," Tony said with lingering amazement. "Marie would have loved that little beach."

"Mm-hmm." She managed the appropriate sound while using him as an unconscious shield.

Behind her, she heard Aaron's voice still going, still loud. "Best excursion ever, am I right?"

And Jerome's quieter response, lost in the sound of passengers streaming back to the ship and the distant beat of Dominican music from the port's speakers.

The gangway stretched before her, leading back to the floating world where she was paid to perform. Ronnie moved forward with the crowd, her shoulders drawing up toward her ears, her arms crossing over her chest. She'd find an empty corner of the ship. She'd spend the evening staring at nothing.

The walls she'd started to let down were going back up.

Higher this time.

Strong enough that no one would get through again.

Five

Ronnie pressed her ear against the cabin door, listening for footsteps in the corridor. The ship had been docked in St. Maarten for over an hour, but the hallways still buzzed with passengers heading to their port adventures. She waited for a lull in the noise, then slipped out quickly, heading straight for the stairwell.

Down from Deck 4 to Deck 1, avoiding the elevators where she might run into anyone from the Mingle group. The gangway was crowded but anonymous, exactly what she needed. Within minutes, she was off the ship and into Philipsburg's early morning quiet.

The small Dutch café on Front Street had weathered awnings and mismatched chairs that promised authenticity over tourism. She ordered coffee and a pastry, found a corner table, and opened the paperback she'd grabbed from her cabin. For the first time since yesterday's disaster on that bus ride back from Puerto Plata, she could breathe.

The coffee was strong, the pastry flaky and sweet, and nobody knew who she was or what had happened after Amber Cove.

She was actually starting to relax when a shadow fell across her table.

"Ronnie."

Jerome's voice held relief, edged with what sounded like urgency. She kept her focus on the book, though the lines blurred and her body tightened.

"I've been looking everywhere for you. You disappeared yesterday, and this morning you were already gone when I checked the dining rooms."

"I'm reading." Her voice came out flat, controlled.

"Can we talk? Please?"

She turned a page she hadn't actually read. "There's nothing to talk about."

"Ronnie, please. Just give me five minutes."

She finally looked up, keeping her expression carefully neutral. "I'm enjoying my morning, Jerome. I'd appreciate it if you'd let me continue."

The dismissal was cold, professional. The same tone she used with drunk customers who got too familiar at hotel bars. She gathered her things with deliberate calm, left money on the table, and walked toward the door.

At the threshold, she paused without turning around. "I heard Aaron loud and clear yesterday. The hired help got the message."

She walked out into the Caribbean sunshine, her sandals clicking against the cobblestone street. She'd made it maybe ten paces when his voice stopped her.

"Ronnie, wait! Please, I'm sorry!"

She turned slowly, and whatever control she'd been maintaining cracked at the sight of his desperate expression. "Sorry for what, exactly? Be specific."

He stepped closer, his hands moving helplessly as he searched for words. "For not shutting Aaron down immediately. For letting him say those things. For ..."

"Stop." Her voice cut through his fumbling apology. "You think I care what Aaron said? I've heard worse from better people than him."

"Then what ..."

"Your silence." The words snapped out of her before she could soften them. "After what happened in that cove, after we ..." She drew in a steadying breath while tourists moved past them in a steady flow. "You kissed me like it mattered. Like *I* mattered. And then you let him treat me like a show."

"That's not what I think!"

"But you didn't say that, did you?" Her voice was rising now, and people were starting to stare. "When it mattered, when you could have said 'No, Aaron, she's not just some cruise ship conquest,' you said nothing."

"I tried to ..."

"You spoke so softly that it never reached anyone. That isn't trying, Jerome. That's self-preservation dressed up as effort, and it lets him walk away with his own version of me."

They stood there in the middle of Front Street, the morning sun already hot on their shoulders, tourists flowing around them like water around stones. Jerome's face showed genuine anguish, but Ronnie was past caring about his feelings.

"I know I failed you," he said quietly. "I know I should have been louder, clearer. I was a coward."

"Yes, you were."

"But what we shared yesterday wasn't nothing to me. It wasn't just convenient or entertainment or any of the shit Aaron said."

"Really? Because from where I sat on that bus, it looked exactly like every other vacation fling. Guy gets some action, lets his friends high-five about it, everyone goes home with a story."

"That's not ..." He stopped, took a breath, started again. "You're right. My silence made it look that way. But that's not what it was to me."

"Then what was it?"

"I don't know yet." His voice carried a truth that made her hesitate. "I know that when you kissed me in that hidden pool, it felt like a moment I had been waiting for without knowing it. And I am sorry I failed to protect that. I am sorry I let Aaron's bullshit make you feel like you are not important to me."

She studied his face, looking for the tell that would reveal this as more vacation smooth talking. But his expression was raw, vulnerable in a way that reminded her of their 3 a.m. conversations over soft-serve.

"Give me today," he said suddenly. "One day to prove that you matter to me. That this matters."

"Jerome ..."

"I know I don't deserve it. I know you have every right to tell me to fuck off. But please. Just today."

She stood there, aware of the audience they'd accumulated, aware of the sun climbing higher, aware of her own pulse thudding in her ears. Every smart instinct told her to walk away. But she was so tired of smart instincts.

"This isn't forgiveness," she said finally. "This is one chance. One."

"I'll take it."

"And if Aaron shows up—"

"He won't. This is just us."

She studied him for another long moment, then nodded. "What did you have in mind?"

"There's a beach on the French side. Orient Bay. It's supposed to be beautiful."

Despite herself, she almost smiled. "You researched beaches?"

"I may have asked the concierge for recommendations this morning. For places that would be ... meaningful."

The tension shifted, softened just enough to breathe. Her hurt remained, and her guard stayed in place, but his awkward sincerity had managed to break through a corner of her defenses.

"Fine. But I'm not pretending everything's okay."

"I'm not asking you to."

The taxi ride took thirty minutes, winding from the Dutch side to the French side of the island. They shared the van with three other couples, which limited conversation to observations about the passing scenery. The forced proximity was awkward after their public confrontation, their knees occasionally touching when the driver took curves too fast.

When they finally arrived at Orient Beach, Ronnie's defensive walls wavered at the sheer beauty of it. The water was an impossible shade of turquoise, so clear she could see fish swimming near the shore. White sand stretched in both directions, backed by green hills ... a perfect postcard scene. The beach was alive with activity: colorful umbrellas dotting the sand, music drifting from beachfront restaurants, people playing in the waves.

They found spots at one of the beach clubs, far enough from the speakers that they could talk but still very much in public. The festive atmosphere around them felt surreal after the intensity of their morning confrontation.

"I'm tired of running," she said suddenly, surprising herself. "From myself, from everything."

"Then stop running."

"It's not that simple."

"Maybe it is." His voice was gentle. "Maybe you just need someone to stop running with you."

She finally let herself take him in. He seemed different in this light, less guarded than on their first night aboard. The Caribbean sun warmed his brown skin with hints of gold, and his eyes revealed a mix of hope and worry.

"You want to know why I'm really on this cruise?" The words came out before she could stop them.

"If you want to tell me."

She took a breath, aware of the beach club noise around them, the waiter approaching with drinks, the couple at the next table taking selfies. This wasn't the right place for this conversation, but she was tired of waiting for right places.

"I was famous once."

"Yeah? How famous?" Jerome asked, his tone curious but not pushy.

"I performed under a stage name." The words felt heavy in her mouth. "Riot. I was ... God, this is harder than I thought."

She took a shaky breath, started again. "Pop punk princess. You know the type? Angry girl music for suburban mall kids. 2011 to 2016."

Still no recognition in his eyes, which was both disappointing and relieving.

"Cherry Bomb lip gloss, that was mine. Well, not mine. Nothing was really mine." Her voice cracked slightly. "Everything was manufactured. The anger, the rebellion, all of it. Packaged and sold at Hot Topic."

The waiter set down their drinks. She picked hers up at once, glad to keep her hands busy.

"My manager was this British asshole who ..." She leaned closer so only Jerome could hear over the beach club music. "He thought Americans were playing at punk. Said we could never be real like the UK bands, the Sex Pistols, or whatever. So instead of letting me be authentic, he decided to capitalize on what he called 'American fake rebellion.'"

A jet ski roared past. She used the pause to steady herself, but when she continued, her voice was shaking.

"Mark. His name was Mark. He bleached my hair, told me how to stand, how to sneer. Had forty-year-old men writing my 'fuck the system' songs while I sold lip gloss to thirteen-year-olds who thought I understood them."

"Jesus," Jerome breathed.

"The worst part?" Her laugh was bitter. "I was good at it. Really fucking good. Made millions pretending to be angry about things I'd never experienced. And all these kids, these beautiful, hurting kids, they believed me. They thought I was speaking their truth when I was just ... lying. Every single day, lying."

Jerome shifted closer, their knees touching under the small table. "What happened?"

"I snapped." The words tumbled out faster now. "Eight years ago, Hard Rock Vegas. I went on stage with just my acoustic guitar and played these songs I'd written about what a fraud I was. Called my own audience zombies for buying my shit. Told them they were idiots for believing in me."

Her hands were shaking. She put down her drink before she spilled it.

"They rioted. Obviously. Started throwing things. Someone ..." Her voice caught. "Someone threw my own Cherry Bomb lip gloss at my face. Direct hit. The photo went everywhere."

She could feel tears threatening, but pushed through.

"My boyfriend, Jamie, filmed the whole thing. My complete breakdown. Posted it within hours with ads enabled. 'RIOT LOSES HER MIND.' Eighteen million views. He made money off the worst night of my life."

She waited for Jerome to pull out his phone, to look up the disaster. Instead, he just watched her face with those careful, kind eyes.

"That must have been incredibly lonely."

The simple observation cut through her defenses. "I had no one. My boyfriend counted his YouTube money. My manager, Mark, told people I was unstable and dangerous. The backup singer I called a friend was sleeping with Jamie. Everyone I trusted either took advantage of my downfall or walked away."

"Why did you do it, though? The acoustic songs?"

"Because Riot was killing me." The words came out raw. "Every day, pretending to be this angry rebel while being completely controlled. I couldn't do it anymore. So I killed her instead. Publicly. Messily."

She laughed, and the sound cracked into a sob. "They labeled it a meltdown. Career suicide. But it was the sanest move I ever made. The only honest move."

"And you haven't performed your own music since?"

"Haven't even written any. Haven't ..." She paused, realizing what she was about to admit. "I haven't really laughed either. Not the real kind. Not since before that night. Eight years of being careful, quiet, safe. Hidden."

Around them, the beach club kept its cheerful buzz. A nearby playlist shifted to Bob Marley. A group of women at the bar burst into laughter. The contrast made her confession feel even more surreal.

"You're not going to look it up?" she asked when he continued to just look at her.

"Why would I? You're telling me what actually matters."

"Everyone looks it up. It's the first thing anyone does. They want to see the freak show."

"I'm not everyone." He reached across the table, his fingers finding hers, holding them steady. "And I don't care about Riot. I care about Ronnie. The person sitting here being brave enough to tell me this."

A slow unwinding touched her, an easing she never expected to feel.

"What about you?" she asked. "You said you wanted to do music festivals, change people's lives. Now you're managing a hotel in Colorado Springs. That's not exactly your dream."

He was quiet for a moment, turning his drink glass in slow circles. "I got an offer a few weeks ago. A friend from college is opening a performance venue in Denver. Live music, local artists, the whole thing. She asked if I wanted to help run it."

"That sounds amazing. Why aren't you doing it?"

"Because it's terrifying." His laugh lacked any sign of amusement. "Hotel management is safe. Predictable. I know exactly what every day looks like. A music venue?" He shook his head slowly. "Risk everywhere. Uncertainty everywhere. And if it fails, that's not just a bad quarter—that's everything."

"So you said no?"

"I haven't said anything. The email's just sitting in my inbox." He turned the glass again, watching the amber liquid catch the light. "I keep telling myself I need more information. More time to think it through. But honestly? I think I'm just waiting for the offer to expire so I don't have to make the choice at all."

The admission seemed to surprise him as much as her. He met her eyes with a rueful half-smile. "Sound familiar?"

She looked at him and saw her own patterns reflected back. Both of them had clung to safety, avoiding the very things that frightened them most.

They drank in small pulls, like each sip bought them a moment to breathe. Ronnie's foot tapped against the deck before she could stop it. She set her glass down and rose.

"Let's walk."

Six

They bailed on the beach club section, walking past the last tidy rows of loungers and curated vibes. The music faded, the crowd loosened, and the only soundtrack left was water and wind and their footsteps sinking into sun hot sand.

Ronnie was about to relax when her brain hit the brakes.

The beach ahead looked normal. People swimming. People sunbathing. A volleyball game where everyone was taking it way too seriously.

Then her eyes adjusted.

Tits! A whole lot of exposed tits and flaccid dicks.

"Oh," Jerome said, landing on the same realization with admirable restraint.

They'd drifted into the clothing optional part of Orient Beach, and it was almost aggressively casual. Nobody was performing. Nobody was staring. Just humans, existing without apology.

Ronnie paused, a restless surge building inside her. People here lived without masks or shame. No pretending. No carefully managed persona. Just themselves.

Eight years. Eight years of careful choices, conservative clothes, hiding her tattoos, minimizing herself to avoid recognition. Eight years of being terrified of her own authenticity.

"You okay?" Jerome asked, noticing her stillness.

She wasn't okay. She was having some kind of breakthrough or breakdown; she couldn't tell which. All these naked people living their truth while she'd spent almost a decade hiding hers.

"When did I become afraid of everything?" The question came out harshly, angry at herself more than anything.

"Ronnie ..."

"No, seriously. When did I end up as a person who clings to the safest option every time? Who fills hotel bars with cover songs? Who hides on cruise ships and prays no one connects her to her past?"

The manic energy was building, making her skin feel too tight. Eight years of careful, diminished choices pressing down on her.

She looked around at all the free bodies, then at Jerome, and made a decision that felt both terrifying and necessary.

"I want to show you something." Her hands went to her swimsuit straps. "Something I've been hiding."

"Ronnie, you don't have to ..."

"I know I don't have to. I want to." She pulled down the top of her one-piece, exposing her breasts to the warm Caribbean air. Around them, nobody even glanced their way. She was just another body on a beach full of bodies. "Look."

She expected his eyes to go where most men's would. Instead, Jerome's focus went straight to her waist, to the tattoo she'd been hiding. The punk rock pinup with her blue mohawk, pole dancing on a microphone stand. The obvious cover-up bikini in different, newer ink.

"I got her during peak Riot. She was originally naked." Her voice came out steadier than she expected. "Had the bikini added after everything crashed. Tried to make her respectable, I guess. Cover up the evidence of who I used to be."

Jerome reached out slowly, giving her time to stop him. When she didn't, his fingers traced the outline of the tattoo with unexpected gentleness. Not grabbing, not groping, just acknowledging this piece of her history with careful reverence.

"She's still fierce," he said softly. "Even with the cover-up. Still rebellious."

"You think?" Her voice cracked slightly.

"Look at her face. She's not tamed. She's just wearing a disguise."

His fingers traced the tattoo again, as though he could feel everything she had tried to bury. The intimacy of being topless while he touched the history on her skin, not the skin itself, loosened her in places she did not expect.

A cautious voice rose inside her. Eight years of protecting herself, and she was on the brink of letting it go. Yet his gentle attention to the mark she had long seen as her greatest mistake stirred a rebellious heat that she could not quiet.

"You know what?" She pulled her swimsuit back up, but the feeling of being seen, truly seen, remained. "Fuck it. Fuck being careful. Fuck being safe."

"What do you mean?"

"I mean, I want to do something reckless. Right now. The sort of thing the old me never thought twice about."

She seized his hand and tugged him along the beach, past the volleyball players and the relaxed sunbathers, toward the curve of sand where the palms created a quiet pocket of shade. Her whole body buzzed with the drive to take back what she had lost.

She turned to face him, the manic energy making her feel electric. "I haven't done anything spontaneous in eight years. Haven't taken a single risk that wasn't calculated to be safe."

"Ronnie, you don't have to prove anything ..."

"I'm not proving anything. I'm remembering."

She kissed him, nothing like the cautious kiss in the hidden cove, but fierce and sure. The way he had looked at her tattoo and touched it with respect instead of judgment had opened a place inside her she had kept sealed for years. Her hands slid beneath his shirt, needing the warmth of his skin. He drew her in without hesitation, aware that this moment held more than physical pull.

This was her revolution.

Not need. Not repair. Choice.

She kissed him harder, dragging a sound from the back of her throat as she pressed closer. Her hands swept down his chest and around his back, pulling him in like she'd been starving for contact. He tightened his hold, firm and grounding, and the kiss turned fierce. Urgent. Unapologetic. Eight years of restraint snapping clean in two.

"We need," she gasped against his mouth, "to find somewhere more private. Now."

They stumbled further down the beach, kissing and grasping, both caught in the undertow of her breakthrough. She spotted an old beach palapa, abandoned and half collapsed, but providing enough shelter from view.

"Here," she said, pulling him into the shade.

"Ronnie, we have to be back by four ..."

"Shut up!"

She kissed him again, harder this time, her hands already working at his swim trunks. This wasn't about romance. This was about reclaiming the part of herself that took what she wanted without apologizing.

"I need you," she breathed against his mouth, pulling him free from his trunks while they stayed around his hips. "Right now."

Her back hit the rough bark of a palm tree as he lifted her, her legs wrapping around his waist instinctively. She reached between them, pulling the crotch of her swimsuit to the side with desperate fingers, not bothering to undress, too consumed by the need to feel him.

"Please," she gasped, and then he was pushing inside her, both of them groaning at the connection.

The first thrust made her cry out, her head falling back against the tree. He stilled, worried, but she dug her nails into his shoulders.

"Don't stop," she breathed, the words torn out of her on a wave of need. "Don't you fucking dare."

He thrust again, deeper, and she surged to meet him. The tree's bark dragged at her back through the damp fabric, a small sting that sharpened everything, bright and immediate. His hands gripped her thighs, steady and unyielding, spreading her wider as he found a rhythm that made her vision spark.

"You're so ... oh, FUCK." he groaned against her neck, his teeth grazing her pulse point.

Speech vanished, replaced by the need to cling to him as he fucked her with growing force. The pulled-aside line of her swimsuit pressed into her hip, and his cock filled her with every strong, steady drive. Sand gave under his feet as he found a new angle, and the adjustment brought him against a place inside her that set her whole body blazing.

"There, right there," she managed to gasp, her pussy clenching around him.

The semi-public nature of it all, the risk of being discovered, only heightened every sensation. She could hear voices in the distance, people walking along the beach not far away, and it made her wilder. She bit down on his shoulder to muffle her cries as he pounded into her, each thrust more desperate than the last.

Her orgasm built like a wave, starting deep in her core and spreading outward. When it crashed over her, she had to bury her face in his neck to keep from screaming, her whole body shaking as her pussy pulsed around him. He followed seconds later, groaning her name as he came, his hips jerking against her as he spilled inside her.

They stayed like that for a moment, both trembling, her legs still wrapped around him, his cock still buried inside. The tree bark had definitely left marks on her back. Sand was everywhere; it shouldn't be. Their swimsuits were still technically on but completely disheveled.

When he finally lowered her back to the ground, her legs were so shaky she had to lean against him for support. That's when the laughter started.

She collapsed against Jerome's chest, laughing so hard that tears streamed down her face, not from sadness but from the pure, overwhelming relief of finding herself again.

"Oh my god," she gasped between laughs. "I forgot. I completely forgot I could do this."

"Have sex on a beach?" Jerome asked, breathless and amused.

"Make a choice without overthinking it." She was still laughing, unable to stop, eight years of careful decisions dissolving into wild joy. "Want it and just ... take it. No committee meeting in my head first."

It wasn't the sex itself that had cracked her open. It was the choosing. The reaching. The refusal to let fear run her life for once in eight goddamn years.

He held her as laughter tore out of her in ragged, unstoppable bursts. It hit so hard it bent her forward and shook her whole body, tears streaming as she clung to him just to stay upright. Every time she tried to breathe, another wave ripped loose, louder than the last, and he kept his hands steady on her back, grounding her through the chaos.

The laughter cracked her wide open. It surged through her and faded, leaving her trembling with shallow breaths. When the last unsteady laugh escaped, she felt lighter, as though an old heaviness had finally washed away.

"Feel better?" he asked.

"Yes," she gasped through the laughter. "Oh god, yes. That's already toward the top of my greatest hits sex list."

"Already? Just toward the top?"

"Well, I need to leave room for improvement," she said, still giggling, wiping tears from her eyes. "We have two more days."

He laughed too and drew her closer, neither of them bothering to fix their rumpled clothes right away. "So this happens often?"

They finally began adjusting their clothes when Ronnie felt a problem. She looked down and groaned.

"Oh shit."

"What?"

"We broke my swimsuit." She showed him where the elastic at the crotch had completely given way, leaving a gap that would be impossible to hide. "I can't walk back like this."

Without hesitation, Jerome pulled off his t-shirt. She got a moment to appreciate the way his shoulders and arms moved, muscles flexing as he found the neck hole and started working at it with his hands.

"What are you doing?"

"Making you a skirt." He gripped the fabric and pulled, the sound of tearing cotton loud on the quiet beach. He ripped the neck hole wider, then held it up. "Step in."

"You're destroying your shirt for me?"

"It's just a shirt." He helped her step into it, pulling it up to her waist, where it fell like a tiny sarong, covering the damaged swimsuit. "There. Beach fashion."

She looked down at the makeshift skirt, then up at him, standing shirtless with sand in his hair and such genuine care in his eyes.

"You know what?" She brushed her fingers over the torn fabric. "This is truer to punk than anything I ever wore as Riot. Fast, messy, useful, ripping it so it fits."

"So I'm punk now?"

"You're getting there," she said, only half joking. "Maybe you should take that Denver job. Sounds like it needs someone who knows how to improvise."

A quick change moved through his expression. "Maybe I should."

They fixed everything else as best they could, both sandy and disheveled but glowing. The walk back toward the commercial area felt different. She felt different. Lighter, despite the sand in uncomfortable places. Freer, despite knowing she still had a performance tonight.

"So this is what the rock star life is like," Jerome said, attempting a joke as they reached the line of taxis. "Sex on the beach, breaking all the rules—"

"Stop." She bumped his shoulder with hers, but she was smiling. "I'm not a rock star."

"Sorry, I didn't mean—"

"It's okay. Just ... I'm not Riot anymore. That person is dead, and I'm glad she's gone."

"You're Ronnie."

"I'm Ronnie," she agreed, though even that felt uncertain.

"And Ronnie ... she kicks ass," he reaffirmed.

They caught a taxi back to the ship, still disheveled but no longer caring. She'd been hiding for eight years, but today she'd remembered what it felt like to be visible. To take up space. To want things and take them without apology.

Tonight she'd have to perform at the gala. Tomorrow she'd have to figure out what came next. But right now, sitting in a crowded taxi with sand in her hair and Jerome's hand resting on hers, she felt more herself than she had since the night she destroyed everything.

Seven

The mirror in Ronnie's cabin had become a stranger these past few days. Tonight, she barely recognized the woman staring back at her.

She turned slowly and studied how the burgundy fabric moved with her body. The dress had been an impulse purchase two years earlier, a future version of herself she never quite reached. One shoulder stood completely bare, cutouts carved along her ribs, the fabric clinging before it swept out at her hips. The cherry bomb tattoo on her exposed shoulder caught the warm cabin light and took on a bright pulse.

Her hand moved automatically toward the cardigan draped over her bed. Old habits. Old armor.

"No," she said aloud, surprising herself with the firmness in her voice. "No more hiding."

She reached for the burgundy lipstick and traced it along her mouth with patient precision. The color lit up her skin in the best way. As she studied her reflection, she recognized a shift in how she carried her shoulders and how naturally she claimed the space around her. The confidence from the beach had not been a fleeting burst. It had settled inside her with calm certainty.

The knock at her door came at exactly seven.

Jerome waited in the hallway wearing a cream blazer and navy pants, his open-collar shirt pressed to perfection. He had put real care into getting ready for formal night. Even so, the way he adjusted his stance revealed a flicker of unease.

"Hi," he said, then his eyes traveled the length of her, lingering on the exposed tattoo. "Wow. You look …"

"Shocked the dress still fits after all that soft-serve?" she offered, enjoying the way his composure cracked slightly.

"Beautiful," he finished. "Really beautiful."

He leaned in to kiss her cheek, a gesture both sweet and slightly formal, his nervousness showing through. The brief contact sent warmth spreading across her skin.

"So," he said, recovering with a small smile, "I thought I'd offer my services as personal security for tonight's performance."

She laughed, the sound escaping like it didn't ask permission. "Are you applying for the job?"

"I can be terrifying on request."

The humor in his eyes was real, but so was the way he kept track of the space around her, like he'd already decided it was his responsibility.

Heading toward the Topaz Lounge, an older woman in the corridor clocked Ronnie's tattoo and pulled a face like Ronnie had personally offended her. The familiar urge to square up sparked hot and fast, but Ronnie swallowed it. She wasn't giving strangers free real estate in her head anymore.

"You okay?" Jerome asked quietly, having noticed the exchange.

His arm wrapped around her waist, his hand finding the bare skin exposed by the dress's cutout. The touch was both protective and intimate.

"I'm fine," she said, then smiled. "Actually fine, not performing fine."

Formal night had given the Topaz Lounge a makeover. Crystal glittered. Dresses shimmered. Jackets fit too well. The room was full of couples and clinking glasses and the gentle, pleased hum of people who had eaten well and started saying yes to one more drink.

Ronnie set up in the corner they'd designated as a small performance space, her guitar case familiar in her hands despite the formal setting. Jerome took his usual spot against the back wall, their unspoken ritual now comfortable as breathing.

She started with a jazzy opener she trusted, smooth enough to make people nod along without thinking about it. The next song was a classic, and suddenly there were dancers, slow and sweet, making the lounge feel smaller. The stage was the one place she never had to explain herself. Her fingers owned the strings, and her voice stayed rich, measured, and fully under her command.

But she'd chosen "The Scientist" deliberately for her third song. The Coldplay piece was about mistakes and longing, about wanting to go back to the start. As the opening chords rang out, she found Jerome's eyes across the room and held them.

"Nobody said it was easy," she sang, her voice carrying through the intimate space. "No one ever said it would be this hard."

She was not performing in the old sense. This was Veronica 'Ronnie' Mills, singing to him with the honesty she could not speak.

Around her, the room eased into a slow sway, and couples drew closer, but her gaze stayed fixed on Jerome. He looked at her as if he had uncovered a rare truth.

She played for over an hour after that, weaving through her repertoire of classics and contemporary covers, upbeat numbers that sent people off into the night with smiles. But nothing matched the intensity of that one song, that one held gaze across the crowded room.

When her set ended, applause rose warm and unforced. People drifted out in small groups, chasing nightcaps and brighter rooms, until the lounge thinned to shadows and half-finished drinks. Jerome didn't move.

"Need help?" he asked, gesturing to her equipment.

"You just want to touch my guitar," she teased, but handed him the cable she'd just coiled.

They worked together, their movements finding an easy rhythm. She was hyperaware of him in the empty lounge, the way his jacket pulled across his shoulders when he bent to collect a microphone stand, how his fingers brushed hers when she passed him another cable.

"You wrap cables like a roadie," she observed, watching his practiced movements.

"Misspent youth," he said with a small smile. "Had a friend with a band in college. Spent a lot of late nights doing exactly this."

"Let me guess, you were the responsible one who made sure everyone got home safe."

"Someone had to be."

She bent to secure her guitar case, fingers fumbling with the latches. Jerome stepped in like it was the most natural thing in the world, his hands steady where hers weren't. The scent of him hit her on a quiet inhale, warm wood and sun.

When she straightened, he was right there. Close enough that she had to lift her chin to find his eyes.

His fingertips found her jaw first, light as a question. Then he dipped his head and kissed her, soft and quick, like a promise he refused to make too loudly. When he pulled back, his thumb brushed along her jawline, and her breath caught on the way out.

She felt heat rise to her cheeks, grateful for the dim lighting.

"I know a spot that has amazing ice cream," he said, his thumb still tracing the line of her jaw, slow and deliberate, like he was memorizing its curve.

She laughed. "At this hour? In formal wear?"

"Especially in formal wear."

The ship had gone hushed in that late-night way, corridors dimmer, footsteps softened by carpet and distance. Ronnie's heels still clicked, crisp against the quiet. Jerome walked close enough that his hand found her lower back in passing, warm contact that lingered just long enough to register.

The soft-serve machine on Deck 10 hummed like it was proud of itself, dispensing perfectly without a single dramatic pause.

They took a small table and ended up closer than usual, knees touching beneath it. Ronnie kicked off her heels and let her bare feet drift forward until they brushed the polished leather of his dress shoes.

"You were different tonight," he said. "When you were singing."

"Different how?"

"Like you meant it. Every word."

She took a thoughtful bite of her vanilla soft-serve. "That song always catches me off guard. It carries that urge to reach back for the moment before everything changed."

"Can't go back, though," he said gently. "Only forward."

"Maybe forward is better." She looked at him directly. "Maybe I needed these eight years to become someone who could handle being seen again."

Before he could respond, heavy footsteps stumbled onto the deck. Aaron appeared, clearly drunk, his bow tie undone and hanging loose around his neck.

"Jerome!" he called too loudly. "Missed karaoke, bro! You should've heard this one guy butcher 'My Way.'"

Aaron dropped heavily into an empty chair at their table, oblivious to the intimate moment he'd interrupted. His gaze landed on Ronnie, taking in her dress with unfocused appreciation.

"The cruise singer cleans up nice," he said with a sloppy grin. "Looking good tonight."

Ronnie's spine stiffened, but before she could respond, Aaron continued.

"You know what I love about cruise entertainment?" He gestured vaguely with his beer bottle. "Always so available for passenger satisfaction. Part of the whole package, right? Like the midnight buffet but prettier."

The words hit Ronnie like ice water. Her whole body went rigid, shame and anger flooding through her in equal measure.

Jerome stood so quickly his chair scraped against the deck. In one fluid motion, he grabbed Aaron by the collar, hauling him to his feet.

"What the hell?" Aaron sputtered, suddenly sobering.

"Go back to the cabin," Jerome said, his voice low and dangerous. "Go to bed before you cause a scene."

"I was just saying ..."

Jerome's hand stayed at Aaron's shirt, tight enough to mean it. "You're drunk. You're rude. And you're finished. Ronnie is a person, not a performance. You will show respect, or you will leave."

Jerome's voice carried an intensity edged with disappointment, a combination Ronnie had not seen from him until now. Aaron's eyes widened as the alcohol lost its grip for a brief moment.

"Jerome, I didn't mean ..."

"I know you didn't mean it, but you said it anyway." Jerome's voice softened just a fraction, but his grip remained firm. "You're better than this, Aaron. So be better. Now go sleep it off before you say something else you'll regret in the morning."

"Jesus, okay, sorry," Aaron mumbled when Jerome released him, genuine embarrassment replacing drunken bravado. "I'm sorry, Ronnie. That was ... I'm an idiot."

He stumbled away, clearly shaken by his friend's reaction.

Jerome stayed on his feet, breathing so calm it made Aaron look even worse by comparison. When he sat again, Ronnie's gaze lingered, not impressed exactly. More... shaken in a way she didn't want to name.

"You just ..." she started, then stopped, her eyes bright with unshed tears. "Thank you."

Understanding dawned in his eyes. The connection to their conversation in St. Maarten, to the wound she'd shared about being laughed at, dismissed, and made into entertainment for others' consumption.

"Just ... thank you," she repeated, her voice thick with emotion. "For seeing me as worth defending."

"Of course I do." He leaned in and took her hand. "You're not entertainment, Ronnie. You're not a product for anyone to claim and discard. You're ..."

He paused, searching for words, but she squeezed his hand.

"I know," she said softly. "I'm starting to know."

The soft-serve had melted into milky soup, forgotten. They sat in the warm night air, the ship gently rocking, neither wanting to break the moment.

"I should probably go," she said eventually, not moving.

"Probably," he agreed, not moving either.

"It's late."

"Very late."

Her foot found his under the table again. The simple touch felt charged with everything that had happened between them since St. Maarten.

"This whole day," she said softly. "The beach, and then tonight, and what you just did with Aaron ..."

She trailed off, the meaning stuck somewhere behind her teeth. He didn't ask her to finish it. He just rose, slow and deliberate, and offered his hand.

When she took it, he drew her up and in, closing the distance like it had been there too long. His palm settled against the bare strip at her waist where the dress dipped away, warm skin to skin, and her breath hitched.

They stood there on the deck with their melted ice cream forgotten on the table, the ship's lights casting shadows across the water. She had to tilt her head back to look at him properly, this man who'd somehow found her behind all her careful walls.

"I don't want tonight to end," she said quietly.

Eight

The door clicked shut, and the world narrowed to this room. No lounge. No corridors. No watching eyes.

Ronnie turned the bedside light down until the space was washed in amber, warm and low, like a secret.

"I want to see you," she said simply, as if saying it plain made it easier to be true.

The small space felt sacred now. Her guitar rested in the corner, red lipstick still on the vanity, sheet music scattered across the desk. Jerome's hands framed her face, thumbs tracing her cheekbones making her breath catch.

"I've been thinking about this," he admitted, his voice rough with honesty. "All through dinner. Longer."

She smiled, that confident spark returning. "Only since dinner? I'm losing my touch."

They came together slowly. This wasn't the urgent desperation of the beach.

This was choosing. This was offering her whole self and trusting him to handle her carefully.

His hands moved to her hair, fingers threading through the soft waves as her own hands found the buttons of his cream blazer. She pushed it off his shoulders, letting it fall to the floor. The formality of their dinner clothes felt like armor they were finally ready to shed.

Her burgundy dress from formal night clung to her curves, the one-shoulder design elegant and complex. His fingers found the hidden zipper at her side, drawing it down with agonizing slowness while his mouth pressed kisses to her exposed shoulder.

The mermaid silhouette held her until the very last inch, then released her all at once.

She stepped out of it carefully, the fabric pooling around her feet like spilled wine.

She unfastened him slowly, button by button, until the barrier between them gave way. His heartbeat steadied beneath her touch as she slid the shirt from his shoulders. He carried strength without performance, the kind that didn't ask to be admired but still was.

When she reached for his belt, her fingers toyed with the buckle, unhurried. Then she let her hand drift lower to cup him through the navy dress pants. The thick, unmistakable shape of his cock pressed hot against her palm, straining beneath the fabric. She squeezed lightly, then stroked along the length, feeling the heat and weight of him. His breath caught, eyes fluttering closed as a low groan rumbled from deep in his chest.

They undressed slowly until they were left with only undergarments and the hush. The dress had left faint marks on her skin. Jerome traced them with gentle fingers, and she went still, letting the touch say what she couldn't.

She could feel the heat radiating from his body, could smell his cologne mixed with arousal.

He lifted her onto the small desk, the wood cool against the backs of her thighs as sheet music fluttered to the floor. Face-to-face now, her legs locked around his waist, drawing him closer until the thick, rigid length of his cock pressed insistently against her through the thin barrier of fabric.

The friction jolted through her, a sharp gasp tearing from her throat as her pussy clenched, hot and needy.

The ache between her legs deepened, a slow, coiling burn that demanded more.

He kissed her like they had all the time in the world. Deep, unhurried, searching. Tongues tangling. Breathing each other in until she felt dizzy with it.

His mouth trailed lower, following the line of her jaw, the slope of her throat, the delicate hollow at the base of her neck. Then the valley between her breasts, his lips warm and wet, his tongue circling lazy patterns over the rise of her cleavage. The gentle scrape of his teeth made her shiver.

The ship rolled beneath them, slow and steady, the engines' low vibration rising through the desk and into her bones. It synced with the rush in her blood, with the ache and heat pooling between her thighs.

Her hands fisted in his hair, holding him there, urging him lower. She arched against him, grinding forward, desperate to feel him harder, closer.

The lace of her panties clung wet to her, soaked through. She felt the answering heat and hardness straining against his boxer briefs, the thick length of him rubbing perfectly where she needed it most. Every pass made her hips buck, made her breath catch.

But he was determined to take his time, to worship rather than conquer.

His hands moved up her back, finding the clasp of her bra with practiced ease, and she let him remove it, let him see all of her in the golden light.

"Fuuuck," he breathed, looking at her like she was art, like she was precious.

His hands cupped her breasts, thumbs brushing over her nipples until they peaked hard and sensitive.

He carried her to the bed and laid her down on crisp white sheets. The cabin faded until there was only the bed, the warmth, the sound of their breathing. His gaze pinned her, slow and starving. It went straight through her.

Kneeling beside her, he began at her ankles, his hands warm and steady as they slid upward. Each pass of his palms left a trail of heat that seemed to sink straight into her bones. By the time he reached her thighs, she could feel her pussy pulsing with want, wetness pooling, every nerve begging for him to touch her there.

He stopped at the delicate lace of her panties, fingertips teasing just along the edges. His gaze lifted to meet hers, silent but clear in its question.

She answered without words, lifting her hips in offering.

He hooked his fingers under the waistband and drew the panties down, slow enough that the lace grazed along her slick folds. His eyes never left hers as he bared her completely.

Now she was bare in a way that had nothing to do with nudity. The vulnerability came from the trust she surrendered, the trust that let him see and touch every part of her without her walls. She saw the moment he felt the full meaning of it. His hands relaxed with care while his eyes deepened with desire.

His fingers traced her hip bones, the soft skin of her inner thighs, everywhere except where she needed him most.

His mouth traced the same path, starting at her ankles, brushing soft kisses up her calves, the inside of her knees. By the time he reached the tender skin of her inner thighs, her breathing had turned shallow, and anticipation coiled tight in her belly.

He spread her legs with patient pressure, opening her to him completely. The first stroke of his tongue over her clit made her gasp, her back arching off the bed.

He didn't rush. He teased with slow passes, then slowed again, drawing it out until her breath started to break. Every time she made a sound, he responded, learning exactly what wrecked her.

Her fists tightened in the sheets as his mouth worked her with unhurried precision.

His lips closed over her clit, drawing it gently before releasing, then his tongue flattened to lap over her, hot and wet, making her hips jerk forward. A feather-light scrape of teeth had her moaning, her thighs tightening around his head.

She had never been so thoroughly attended to, so completely made the center of someone's hunger.

This was worship.

He gave her everything. Lips coaxing, tongue flicking, teeth grazing. Until her entire body trembled, the pleasure building and building, her muscles tight with the need to come. Every time she hovered on the edge, he slowed, pulling her back, stretching the moment until she was aching for release.

When she couldn't take it anymore, when the tension in her body was so sharp it felt like breaking, she reached for him, pulling him up to her mouth.

"Please," she breathed against his lips, tasting her own slickness on his tongue.

He shoved his boxer briefs down and kicked them away. Her eyes dropped instantly, drinking in the sight of him. His cock was thick and hard, the head flushed and gleaming. She wrapped her fingers around him, feeling the solid weight, the heat radiating against her palm. He was heavy and perfect, filling her hand.

He groaned at her touch, his hips jerking forward involuntarily.

He positioned himself above her, supporting his weight on his forearms so he could see her face. When he finally pushed inside her, sliding his cock into her wet heat with agonizing slowness, they both went perfectly still.

The sensation was overwhelming, not just physical but emotional, the feeling of being completely connected to another person.

She was tight around him, her pussy clenching greedily, as if her body already knew it never wanted to let him go. The first deep push had her nails biting into his shoulders, her breath catching at the stretch, the exquisite fullness.

"You okay?" he asked, his voice rough, strained with the effort it took not to lose control.

"More than okay," she whispered, her legs locking around his waist to pull him deeper. She welcomed every inch, tilting her hips to take him as far as he could go.

They started slow, bodies syncing without effort. Instinctive and patient. He withdrew just enough to make her whimper before sliding back in, his cock gliding right through her slick heat.

Her pussy gripped him on every thrust, the head of his cock finding that spot inside her that made her gasp, made her vision spark. Every movement fed the hunger coiling low in her belly, each push sending pleasure radiating outward in waves.

She wrapped her arms around him, pressing her chest to his, skin to skin, his heartbeat pounding against her own. He filled her completely consuming her, until she couldn't tell where she ended and he began.

When the angle was not quite right, when she wanted more control, she pressed her palms to his chest.

"Let me," she murmured, and he let her guide him onto his back.

She moved down his body, taking his cock in her mouth, tasting both of them on his skin. His groan was deep, his head falling back, one hand finding her hair. She worked him slowly, learning what made him gasp, what made his hips lift from the bed.

When she finally moved back up, she guided him to her entrance and sank down until he filled her completely.

They both groaned together. She stilled for a moment, savoring the stretch, the way his cock throbbed inside her.

Up here, she was in charge. Period. She could go slow. She could go ruthless. She could change her mind mid-breath.

She began with a deliberate, unhurried roll, just to watch his face when she did it. The look he gave her made heat lick up her spine. His hands followed, equal parts worship and restraint, bracing her when she picked up speed like he'd decided he'd rather hold on than try to stop her.

The friction of her clit against his pelvis sent jolts of pleasure through her, each movement winding her tighter. She moved with more intent now, chasing the building rush, and he met her thrust for thrust, his hands guiding but never controlling.

She felt the orgasm building, the pleasure starting as a tight coil in her clit and then spreading outward through her whole body like ripples on water.

"Jerome," she gasped, and he understood. He sat up, wrapping his arms around her as she broke apart in his hold. Her pussy clenched around his cock, gripping him as wave after wave of pleasure crashed through her, each one wringing a sharp cry from her throat until it became a hoarse moan.

But he was not finished with her yet.

He eased her onto her side, moving with her, entering her again from behind. The wet heat welcomed him easily, the angle pushing him deeper than before. His arm tightened around her waist, his mouth hot against her neck. She could feel every inch of him moving within her, the deep, slow grind making her gasp with each stroke.

His free hand cupped her breasts from behind, squeezing them in his palms, thumbs brushing her nipples until they were hard and aching. He rolled and tugged at them while he fucked her, each rough pinch pulling a sharp sound from her lips.

"I can't ..." she started, but it broke into a whimper as his fingers left her nipples and slid between her thighs. He found her clit and circled it slowly, while his cock filled her over and over.

The sensations tangled together, impossible to separate. Her pussy gripped him tighter, the wet suction drawing a low, guttural sound from his chest. Her own cries grew louder, more desperate, the pleasure mounting with brutal inevitability.

When it hit, it tore through her like lightning. She screamed his name, her voice raw, her body locking around him as the orgasm ripped her apart. Her legs shook, her hips jerking helplessly as her pussy milked his cock.

He groaned against her neck, his thrusts turning urgent, deep, until he was buried to the hilt and spilling inside her. The hot rush of his release filled her as his body tensed, another deep, almost feral sound breaking from his throat. He stayed pressed tight against her, grinding slowly through the aftershocks until they were both shaking.

They lay still afterward, hearts pounding, skin slick with sweat despite the air conditioning.

He was still inside her, still holding her close, and she never wanted him to let go.

The ship rocked them gently as their breathing slowly returned to normal. She could hear the distant sounds of the ship at night, the hum of machinery, the occasional footstep in the corridor, but it all felt far away, irrelevant to this perfect bubble they had created.

Eventually, he slipped out of her, but he didn't move away. Instead, he gathered her closer, pulling the sheet over them both. She turned in his arms so she could see his face in the dim light.

"That was ..." she started, then stopped, not sure how to finish.

"Yeah," he agreed softly, understanding perfectly.

She nodded, tracing lazy circles on his chest with her fingertip. "I didn't know it could feel like that."

He pressed a kiss to the top of her head.

"I'm honored," he said simply, and she knew he meant it.

They lay in the aftermath, woven together beneath the sheet, fingers threaded as if that simple contact could hold the world steady. The quiet around them felt earned, not awkward. Like the room itself was letting them rest.

Ronnie felt changed in a way that had nothing to do with skin. The pleasure had been breathtaking, yes, but the real tremor ran deeper, into the places she kept locked and labeled off limits. Something inside her had swung open.

A last defense had slipped.

She sensed the turn in him in small things. The faint hitch in his hand where it moved through her hair. The way his breath went careful. When she looked up, she found a new set to his mouth, a crease between his brows.

Concern, plain as a bruise.

"Ronnie," he said eventually, his voice careful, weighted with whatever he'd been turning over in his mind.

She tensed slightly at his tone. She'd heard that voice before, the one that came before bad news. "What?"

His fingers stilled in her hair. "I need to tell you something. About that night."

Her body went rigid. "What night?" But she already knew.

"In Vegas. I was there."

The words hit her like cold water. She pulled away from him, sitting up abruptly, clutching the sheet to her chest. "What do you mean, you were there?"

He sat up too, reaching for her, but she was already moving. She swung her legs over the side of the bed, putting physical distance between them; the sheet wrapped around her like she was using it for protection. The cabin suddenly felt too small, the walls pressing in.

"I wasn't inside during your show," he said to her back. "I was working security that night. College money, you know? Post-show cleanup, crowd control, keeping people away from backstage. There were maybe fifteen of us on the crew."

She didn't turn around. Her mind raced, trying to process this impossible coincidence. "You saw the show?"

"No. I came in after. After the cameras stopped rolling, after most everyone cleared out." He hesitated. "We were breaking down barricades near the stage. That's when I saw you."

The memory crashed over her. That stage. Sitting among the destroyed equipment and burned merchandise, makeup running, everything in ruins. The complete breakdown she thought no one had witnessed.

"You saw that?" Her voice was small, horrified.

"I saw a woman who looked broken but fierce," he said carefully. "A woman fighting through an experience no one should have to face."

She rose and walked to the small vanity, needing a steady surface beneath her hands. Her reflection met her in the dim light, flushed and disheveled, every emotion too close to the surface. She gripped the edge until her fingers tightened with strain.

"When I told you on the beach." She couldn't look at him. "Did you already know? Was everything after that just you closing some loop from eight years ago?"

"No." The bed creaked as he adjusted. "I didn't realize it was you until you said your name. You look nothing like that old version of yourself. Riot had bleached hair and heavy makeup. She was not the woman I see now."

"But you still reacted like you'd known all along." She turned, gaze locked on his. "You said my voice sounded lived-in. You weren't shocked when I told you."

Jerome held her stare for a second, then looked away like he didn't deserve to. "When you started talking on the beach, the pieces started to fit." He paused. "Then you said the name, and I..." His hand went to his face, rubbing hard. "I panicked. Because what do you say to someone who's finally trusting you with that? How do you tell them you were there without making it about you? I didn't want to do that. Not to you."

"So you just said nothing."

"I didn't know how to say it without making it worse. Without making it seem like I had some claim on your pain."

She stared at him, processing this. "So what, I was just some celebrity conquest? Some broken girl you could finally get close to?"

"No." His voice was firm now. "Ronnie, I swear to you."

"Everyone always wants the story." Her tone went flat, clipped. A retreat. "The tragedy. The scandal. The girl who threw it all away."

"I don't want your story." He stood slowly, but didn't approach her. Gave her the space she was demanding. "I didn't want to center myself in your pain. That night wasn't mine to claim. I was just there. A witness. That's all."

"What else did you see?"

He hesitated, eyes searching her face like he was checking for fractures.

"You kept trying to play," he said. "I was far enough away that you were mostly silhouette and motion, but I could still see it. The shake in your hands. The way you'd start, stop... then fold over the guitar like it was a life vest."

Her throat tightened. Nobody knew about the guitar. Not the tabloids. Not the documentary crews. Not anyone.

"I could see your shoulders hitching like you'd been sobbing," he added. "Your face looked smeared, like you'd dragged your hands across it." His voice dipped. "And you kept speaking to empty air. Your lips were moving like you were answering someone who wasn't there."

She turned away from him again, pressing her palm flat against the cool surface of the vanity. The memory was there, vivid and sharp. Her lips moving, the same words over and over like a prayer or a curse.

"I wasn't ready for this," she whispered.

"What?"

"That is what I kept saying." She looked at him at last, eyes glistening. "I was not ready for this. I was not ready for everything to fall apart all at once." Her voice faltered. "I thought I had more time. To understand myself. To become a person shaped by my own choices, not theirs."

He did not move toward her, but his expression softened with clear recognition. "You were so young."

"Then Mark came back." She hugged herself, the sheet slipping slightly. "He was furious. Screaming at me. Calling me ungrateful, saying I'd destroyed everything he built."

"I saw him grab that cymbal stand and just launch it. Missed your head by inches."

"I didn't even flinch." She laughed, but there was no humor in it. "I was so far gone I didn't even care if it hit me."

"You were in shock." His voice was quiet. "After he stormed off, I wanted to go up there. Check on you, I don't know, do something. But my supervisor grabbed my arm. Said, 'Don't even think about it. Said approaching the talent is how lawsuits happen, how people lose their jobs.' So I just—" He stopped, and she heard something raw in his voice. "I just stood there. Watched you sit alone on that stage until someone finally came to get you. And I've thought about that night more times than I can count. Wondering if I should have ignored him and gone up anyway."

The tears came then, sudden and hot, sliding down her cheeks before she could stop them. She sank down onto the small chair by the vanity, suddenly exhausted by the weight of it all.

"I was so angry," she whispered. "At him. At myself. To everyone who told me I should be grateful for the cage they built around me."

He moved then, slowly, giving her time to stop him. When she didn't, he knelt in front of her, not touching, just present.

"Everyone said I was the villain," she continued, her voice thick. "That I bit the hand that fed me. That I was crazy, unstable, a cautionary tale."

"They were wrong."

She lifted her gaze through her tears, toward the man who had seen her most painful truth and still understood more than the shame. "Do you think I'm crazy for destroying it all?"

"I think you're brave as hell."

The words landed somewhere deep in her chest, in a place she'd kept locked for eight years. She studied his face, looking for any flicker of judgment, any sign that now he knew the whole story, he might see her differently.

"Even knowing how messy it got? How I completely fell apart?"

His hand found hers, gentle, asking for permission. She let him take it.

"Especially then." His thumb traced across her knuckles. "You didn't fall apart. You survived. There's a difference."

She remained silent, allowing his words to move through her. He had met her in a moment of raw collapse, alone and grasping her guitar for any sense of stability. Yet he carried away an image marked by strength, not ruin.

"Why didn't you ever watch the video?" she asked finally. "Everyone else did. Millions of people."

"I saw enough that night," he said, voice even but edged. "Enough to know it wasn't a performance. It was a collapse, and people were filming it like it belonged to them." He shook his head. "I didn't need a replay."

A new clarity unfolded inside her, as if an inner latch had finally eased open. She stood and stepped toward him. He rose in the same breath, and when she pressed against him, his arms closed around her with a welcome that felt inevitable.

"This is insane," she murmured against his skin. "The odds of this. You being there. Us ending up on the same cruise eight years later."

"I know." His chin rested on top of her head. "I've been trying to do the math. It doesn't add up."

"I don't believe in fate."

"Neither do I."

"Then what is this?"

He rubbed his thumb over her knuckles once. "Maybe it's just that. Two people who needed to find each other." He huffed a quiet breath. "No cosmic reason. Just luck."

"I don't want to leave this cabin," she murmured.

"We don't have to."

Nine

Smooth, familiar curves met her hands in the dark, settling against her bare hip with a weight that steadied her. For a moment, she let herself pretend it was something simpler. Skin. Warmth. A body she could trust without thinking.

She traced slowly, as if relearning a language she'd never actually forgotten. The shape beneath her palms felt intimate in the way only familiarity can be, something she knew down to the smallest details. Her fingertips found the lines by instinct, following them with unhurried purpose, mapping what she already belonged to.

There were places worn softer than the rest, edges polished by years of touch. She found one spot where the finish had thinned, where everything felt impossibly smooth, almost tender. Her thumb lingered there, stroking once, then again, and her breath hitched like her body expected an answer.

A small sound slipped out of her before she could stop it.

Her thumb dragged slowly across what was drawn tight beneath her hand.

It responded immediately. A low vibration bloomed against her palm, humming up into her skin like a pulse. She pressed down, holding it there, letting the resonance thrum through her as if she could borrow steadiness from it. As if she could keep herself together by sheer contact.

She shifted closer, pulled it in tighter, cheek near the curve, breathing in the faint scent that lived in the dark. Salt air clinging to everything aboard the ship. A trace of wood. Something comforting and known.

G major. The first position she'd ever learned.

C. Then D. The progression so ingrained she could do it dreaming, fingers moving even when her mind tried to drift away.

Only then did the truth surface, quiet and unavoidable.

Her fingers began to move with more intention, coaxing out a melody. Notes she hadn't played in eight years, rising from some locked room in her chest. The opening bars of "Glitter and Gasoline" filled the air around her, fragile as spun glass.

She hummed along. Just breath and melody. Testing whether her voice still remembered the shape of these songs.

It did.

The first verse slipped out in a near whisper. She had written these lyrics at nineteen, angry and raw and desperate to be heard. They tasted different now. The bitterness had eased. They worked like a hard swallow of medicine, sharp as they went down yet healing in a deeper place.

She played through the chorus, her voice finding edges that hadn't been there in years. The edges that had once made crowds scream and record executives salivate, and Mark pushed her harder, harder, always harder until she shattered.

But this wasn't for them.

This was hers.

Her fingers jumped to "Cherry Bomb Heart." Then "Riot Act."

And then there was no stopping it. Song after song, spilling out like testimony, her voice settling into something clear and dangerous. The guitar heated where it touched her, buzzing under her palms, a live wire she knew how to hold.

Then the opening riff of "Only Posers Die."

The song that had ended everything.

The song that had maybe, she was starting to realize, saved her too.

Tears slid down her cheeks. She could feel them but not see them. Could taste the salt when they reached her lips. But she didn't stop playing. Her voice cracked on the bridge, held steady on the final chorus.

These songs had been held captive for eight years. She had locked them away because they hurt too much, because the world had twisted them into an ugly story, because she had allowed other people's versions of that night to decide what her music meant.

No more.

When the last chord faded, she sat in the silence and let herself feel the weight of what she'd just done.

A soft click. Then the amber light flooded the tiny cabin.

She blinked, eyes adjusting. Jerome was propped on one elbow across the small space, sheet pooled at his waist, watching her with an expression she couldn't read. Tender. Awed. Maybe a little heartbroken.

The cabin snapped back into focus around her. The rumpled bed. The narrow desk. Jerome.

She'd forgotten he was there.

She became suddenly aware of herself—perched on the small chair, naked except for the guitar across her lap, tears drying on her cheeks, hair wrecked from sleep and sex and whatever emotional excavation the last hour had been.

"Well," she said. "This is a look."

"It's a good look." His voice was sleep-rough but amused. "Very VH1 Behind the Music."

"How long have you been awake?" Her voice came out rough, scraped raw from singing.

"Since 'Cherry Bomb Heart.'" He didn't move toward her. Seemed to understand this moment required stillness. "I was pretending to be asleep so you wouldn't stop."

She looked down at the guitar in her hands. The same guitar she'd clutched on that Vegas stage eight years ago. The only witness, she thought, when everything fell apart.

"I think I want to play tonight." The words came slowly, like she was discovering them as she spoke. "Not covers. My songs."

"I know." His voice was quiet. Certain. "I could hear it."

She met his eyes. "I'm scared."

"Bullshit." A grin spread across his face. "You literally did this in front of fifteen thousand people. Multiple times. For money."

"That was different."

"How?"

"I don't know. It just was." She hugged the guitar against her chest. "What if I'm not good anymore?"

"Ronnie. You just played a private concert naked and crying, and it was still the best thing I've ever heard." He raised an eyebrow. "Tonight you'll have clothes on. You're already ahead."

She snorted. "That's your pep talk? At least I'll be wearing pants?"

"Pants, no tears, maybe some mascara that stays on?" He ticked them off on his fingers. "Standing ovation. Guaranteed."

"You're an idiot."

"And yet you're smiling."

She was. Dammit.

"What if I bomb?"

"Then you bomb in front of a hundred drunk people on a boat in the middle of nowhere, and none of them will ever see you again." He shrugged. "Honestly, it's kind of the ideal place to have a meltdown. Very low stakes."

She threw a pillow at him. He caught it, laughing.

"I'll be there," he said, softer now but still warm. "Heckling from the back if you need a confidence boost."

"My hero."

"I do what I can."

She set the guitar carefully back in its case and crossed to the bed, letting him pull her down against his chest. His arms came around her, solid and warm.

"Thank you," she murmured against his skin. "For letting me have that."

"Are you kidding?" His chest rumbled beneath her cheek. "Naked dawn concert? That's the kind of thing you shut up and appreciate."

She laughed into his shoulder. "You're ridiculous."

"You like it."

She really, really did.

They stayed where they were while the ship gathered momentum around them. Footsteps moved past the door. A service cart rolled by, its wheels complaining. A tinny announcement seeped through the wall, smoothed by distance into a low, constant murmur.

Tonight was farewell night.

Tonight, Riot would rise.

The Topaz Lounge was packed with their Mingle at Sea group, plus overflow from other passengers drawn by the farewell night energy. Maude stood near the small stage in one of her signature flowing dresses, this one in deep ocean blue that matched her eyes. Her silver-streaked hair caught the ambient lighting as she gestured animatedly to a cluster of regulars.

Jerome took his usual position at the back of the room, their established signal of support. When their eyes met across the crowded space, he gave her the smallest nod.

She was ready.

Maude's voice carried easily over the crowd as she tapped her champagne flute with a fork. "Ladies and gentlemen, if I could have your attention for our farewell toast."

The room gradually quieted, faces turning toward their host with the practiced attention of people who'd learned to trust her guidance over the past six days.

"The ocean has moods," Maude said. "She can throw a fit, then turn around and hold her breath so still you'd swear she's asleep. But she's never done. Even when she looks calm, she's becoming."

She lifted her champagne flute toward the room. "This week, I've watched all of you do the same. I've seen people discover parts of themselves they'd forgotten existed. I've witnessed courage bloom in the most unexpected moments. I've watched travelers become explorers, not just of new places, but of new possibilities."

Tony Castellano wiped his eyes with his napkin, his wedding ring catching the light as he raised his own glass. Around the room, other faces showed the particular vulnerability that came at the end of shared journeys.

"Sometimes the ocean keeps her treasures hidden for years," Maude continued, her voice taking on a distant quality. "Buried beneath layers of sand and salt and time. But when the moment is right, when the current shifts just so, everything that was meant to surface finally breaks free."

Maude looked at Ronnie. The message didn't miss.

"So tonight, as we prepare to return to our regularly scheduled lives, let's remember that the ocean doesn't stop moving just because the voyage ends. The changes you've made this week, the connections you've formed, the truths you've discovered about yourselves ..." She paused, letting the words settle. "Those travel with you wherever you go."

She raised her glass higher.

"To endings that are really beginnings. To the courage to be authentically, completely, unapologetically yourselves. And to our Ronnie, who's been the soundtrack to our transformation all week long."

RIOT AMBER

The room burst into applause, then rolled straight into a messy, joyful toast. Ronnie rode the familiar adrenaline as she headed for the small stage, guitar in hand. Only this time, the energy felt electric instead of sickening.

She settled onto the stool and adjusted the microphone, her movements confident and economical. The room gradually quieted as she began picking out soft, meandering notes on her guitar. Nothing structured, just gentle arpeggios that filled the space while she found her words.

She looked out at the faces watching her. Really looked. Not fans chasing a spectacle. Not executives evaluating her worth. Just people who had spent six days knowing her as Ronnie, no stage name required.

"Thanks for listening to me as Ronnie this week," she said, her fingers still moving across the strings in quiet, thoughtful patterns. "But some of you might remember me from about ten years ago, when I went by Riot."

The reaction was immediate. Gasps from people who suddenly recognized the bone structure beneath her softer styling. Whispers as passengers pulled out phones to confirm what they'd just heard. Someone near the bar dropped their drink. A woman in the front row turned to her husband and smacked his arm repeatedly, mouthing *I told you, I told you*.

Ronnie's fingers kept moving. The notes snapped into a line. Her voice lifted, steadier. Stronger.

"Tonight, Riot is reborn."

The picking pattern evolved, becoming the unmistakable opening of "Glitter and Gasoline."

Her voice reentered the power and range that once owned whole arenas. A new ease settled into her posture as the familiar lyrics took shape. Her shoulders rose with confidence. Her voice filled out, rich and sure.

The performer who'd once commanded thousands of screaming fans began to emerge, transformed but unmistakable.

The crowd was already singing along. Voices joined hers on the chorus, tentative at first, then stronger.

Tony went still, his face moving from puzzled to sure to downright amazed as the melody settled in. He grabbed for his phone, fingers trembling as he hit record. He nudged the person next to him and said in a proud, carrying voice, "My granddaughter is gonna lose her mind."

As the last notes faded, she looked out at the captivated faces. "These songs were born from my anger, my pain, my truth. Tonight, I'm singing them because I'm not angry anymore. I'm free."

Song after song, she owned that stage.

A voice in the crowd shouted, "We love you, Riot!" She grinned, actually grinned, and launched into the next one harder. Her foot tapped against the stool. Her free hand gestured, conducting the energy in the room like she was born for it.

Because she was.

The small space felt electric. People weren't just watching anymore—they were part of it. Swaying, singing, completely caught up in the raw magnetism pouring off the stage.

She rose from the stool mid-song, guitar still in hand, and claimed every inch of the tiny stage. Her voice filled the corners of the room. The Ronnie who had been hiding was gone, replaced by a woman who remembered exactly how good it felt to move people with the truth in her music.

"This is what I was supposed to be doing," she called out between songs, breathing hard, eyes bright. "This is who I am."

The crowd erupted. Jerome stood at the back, hands raised above his head, cheering like he was at Madison Square Garden. She caught his eye, and he shrugged as if to say *what did I tell you?*

An older woman near the stage waved her phone. "My daughter is going to die. She had your poster on her wall!"

"Tell her I said hi," Ronnie grinned. "And that I'm sorry I disappeared for a while."

For her finale, she shifted back to the stool, bringing the microphone closer. The energy in the room was crackling, anticipatory. She let the silence build.

The opening chords of "Only Posers Die" rang out, but the melody had evolved. Softer in places, more defiant in others.

"Eight years ago, I performed this song for the first time," she said, her voice carrying easily over the hushed crowd. "It burned down everything I'd built. Everything they'd built for me."

A voice broke through the noise with, "Burn it down again!" Others laughed and cheered in agreement.

She smiled, a real rock star smile. "But sometimes you have to burn it all down to rise from the ashes. Sometimes destruction is just another word for transformation."

By the chorus, her heel was thumping the footrest like it had somewhere to be. The rhythm climbed into her body and stayed there. Sweat slicked her hairline. The steel strings buzzed under her fingers as she pushed the melody until it stopped asking permission.

She looked up and found Jerome in the crowd. He held her gaze like he'd been there the whole time. Like he wasn't watching a show. He was watching her choose herself in real time.

Her voice soared, and this time the whole room joined in: "Only posers die, but the real ones rise! Truth cuts through the fake like a knife through lies! I burned it all down to find what survives! Only posers die, but the real ones rise!"

The room hit a boil. Bodies pressed closer. Shoes thudded against the deck. People shouted lyrics like they'd been waiting all week for this exact release.

This wasn't nostalgia or novelty. This was artistry, raw and honest and completely alive.

When the last note faded, the silence stretched for three heartbeats.

The room exploded.

Everyone on their feet, shouting, crying, hands in the air. Pure electricity.

Ten

Ronnie sat motionless on the small stage, her guitar in her lap, watching the room tilt into chaos. People swiped at their tears. Phones captured every second. From the bar, a man shouted, "Holy shit, I had no idea!"

The applause kept going. And going.

She'd forgotten what this felt like. Not the manufactured enthusiasm of industry showcases or the polite appreciation of hotel bar crowds. This was real. Raw. People responding to her music, not her image.

"Ronnie!" Maude appeared first, tears streaming down her cheeks. "My dear, that was …" She pressed both hands to her heart, unable to finish.

Then came the rush. Passengers surrounding the stage, talking over each other.

"Your voice is incredible."

"I had chills the entire time."

"Thank you for sharing that with us."

Each comment struck her in a way the usual praise never had. These people knew her. They had spent six days with Ronnie, not the Riot persona that once swallowed everything else. When they said her music was beautiful, they meant it.

She managed to thank them, her voice hoarse from singing and emotions. But even as she graciously accepted their congratulations, her eyes searched the dispersing crowd.

But ... Jerome?

People filtered out in small groups, the room loosening into quiet. Chairs sat skewed. Glasses and crumpled napkins dotted the tables. Ronnie packed her guitar with unsteady hands, adrenaline finally catching up. She'd done it. Actually done it. She'd stepped onstage as herself and walked off still standing.

More than survived. Thrived.

Across the lounge, she spotted Tony sitting alone at a corner table. While everyone else had been celebrating, he'd stayed quiet, phone clutched in his hands, staring at nothing with an expression of pure wonder.

Ronnie pulled the promotional photo from her guitar case. The edges were soft and worn from years of being tucked away, and the corners were slightly bent from travel. She'd signed it earlier in her cabin, thinking about his stories of Sophia and the Cherry Bomb lip gloss that had made a struggling teenager feel brave every morning.

"Tony?" She approached his table. "I thought Sophia might like this."

He looked up at her, then down at the photograph. His hands trembled as he accepted it, reading the inscription she'd written: *To*

Sophia, Never apologize for taking up space. Fuck the haters. Stay loud. Love, Riot.

"You're ..." His voice cracked. "All this time, you were ..."

"A friend." Ronnie smiled. "Sophia has excellent taste in music."

Tony looked down at the photo, then back at her, understanding dawning in his eyes. "All this time, I've been telling you about her ..."

"She sounds like an amazing young woman. You should be proud."

"Thank you." His voice was quiet, sincere. "She's going to love knowing I actually got to talk with you."

As Tony slipped the photo into his jacket pocket, Ronnie spotted Aaron heading their way. The swagger he usually led with had vanished, leaving a surprisingly humble expression in its place.

"Ronnie." He stopped a few feet away, hands shoved deep in his pockets. "I've been a complete ass this week. The way I talked about you, like you were just ... entertainment. That wasn't okay. You're a person, not some cruise ship commodity, and I was threatened by Jerome's obvious feelings for you." He met her eyes directly. "I'm sorry. You didn't deserve any of that shit."

She studied his face, noting the genuine remorse in his expression. "Yes, you're an ass. But at least now you're an ass with insight. So ... progress?"

Aaron blinked, caught off guard by her lack of polish. Then he laughed, low and genuine, like he'd finally decided to stop performing too.

"Okay. Point taken. I deserved that." He rubbed the back of his neck, glancing toward the stage as if it might still be humming. "But what you did up there tonight? That was fearless."

"Okay, I wasn't prepared for your whole redemption arc tonight, Aaron."

They traded a smile that said, without saying it, Well. Look at us. Not fighting for once.

As Aaron turned to leave, she called after him, "Have you seen Jerome?"

"I don't know, I think he snuck out."

Ronnie's stomach dropped. Why would Jerome leave? Tonight, of all nights?

She said quick goodbyes to the remaining stragglers and headed for the elevators. The ship felt different now, like the whole world had shifted while she was on stage. Or maybe she was the one who had shifted.

The top deck was nearly empty when she found him.

Jerome stood at the soft-serve machine like it had personally insulted him. He pressed a button. The machine coughed out a sad ribbon of ice cream, then stopped. Press. Sputter. Stop.

"Come on," he muttered, jabbing another control. "You were fine yesterday."

Ronnie watched his shoulders creep higher, watched his hands do that rare thing where they didn't know what to do next. The steady guy, defeated by a dessert dispenser. He looked exactly like she felt on night one, when the universe decided even ice cream was too much.

She stepped up beside him and gave the machine a firm smack with her palm. Right where he'd shown her earlier in the week.

Perfect soft-serve flowed immediately.

Jerome turned to her, and despite everything, his smile bloomed slowly and appreciative. "Well, look at that. The student becomes the master."

"You looked like you needed some help."

They didn't rush to move away, the machine's soft hum filling the space between them. The deck felt tucked away from the ship's pulse. Most passengers were asleep, or scattered below into lights and music and too-late laughter.

"Why did you leave?" she asked.

Jerome ran a hand through his hair, looking suddenly vulnerable in a way she'd never seen before. "I needed a minute to process what I just witnessed." He gestured vaguely toward the interior of the ship. "That was ... God, Ronnie. That was incredible."

"I thought you'd be proud. Happy for me."

"I am proud. That's exactly the problem." He turned to face her fully. "Watching you up there, seeing what you're capable of ... you could have anything now. Any life you want."

She moved closer, studying his face in the soft deck lighting. "And you think I won't want this? Won't want you?"

Jerome looked away, then back at her, struggling with the words. "I think ..." He stopped, ran a hand through his hair. "I think you might realize you don't need me anymore."

His vulnerable tone reached a place inside her she had kept tightly closed. All week, she had carried the fear and hesitation. Now he was the one facing the same uncertainty.

"Jerome." She reached for his hands. "I'm the same person who's been here all week. The woman who couldn't work an ice cream machine and was too scared to sing her own songs. That's still me."

"But it's not, though." His voice was soft. "You're not hiding anymore. You're not afraid."

"No," she agreed. "I'm not. But that doesn't mean I'm going anywhere."

They returned to the table they had shared on the first night. The comfortable flow of their usual talks was missing. Jerome looked caught inside a thought he had not yet found the courage to share.

"Ronnie." He turned his drink glass in slow circles, a gesture she recognized from the beach in St. Maarten. "That email is still sitting in my inbox."

She didn't need to ask which one. The Denver venue. The dream he'd been too afraid to reach for.

"Has the offer expired yet?"

He shook his head slowly. "She gave me until the end of the month. Said she wanted me to really think about it."

"And have you? Really thought about it?"

"I've thought about nothing else since we talked." He met her eyes. "Watching you tonight, seeing you step into something that terrified you ... it made every excuse I've been telling myself sound pathetic."

"They weren't pathetic. They were safe." She squeezed his hands. "I understand safe. I've been living there for eight years."

"But you're not anymore."

"No. I'm not." She held his gaze. "And neither should you be."

Jerome was quiet, his thumb tracing circles on her palm. "It's still a massive risk. If it fails—"

"Then it fails. And you figure out what comes next." She leaned forward. "Jerome, you just watched me get up on stage and reclaim my entire identity in front of a couple of hundred passengers. You think I'm going to let you hide from this?"

A laugh escaped him, some of the tension leaving his shoulders. "That's not exactly fair. You can't use your big triumphant moment to guilt me into life decisions."

"Watch me." She smiled. "You told me on that beach that you were waiting for the offer to expire so you wouldn't have to choose. But not choosing is still a choice. It's just the wrong one."

He stared at her for a long moment, something shifting behind his eyes. "When did you get so wise?"

"Somewhere between the panic attack and the standing ovation, apparently."

Jerome laughed again, fuller this time. He pulled out his phone, staring at the screen as if it might bite him.

"Right now?" she asked.

"If I don't do it now, I'll talk myself out of it by morning." He looked up at her. "Stay with me?"

She nodded, moving her chair closer so their shoulders touched.

He opened the email, typed for a long moment, then angled the screen toward her.

I'm in. Call me Monday.

"Send it," she said.

He clicked.

Silence, not empty but stunned. Like their bodies needed a second to catch up to what they'd just agreed to. They had spent years choosing the smaller option. Tonight, they didn't.

"So," Jerome said, a new energy in his voice. "I guess I'm opening a music venue in Denver."

"I guess you are."

"Which means I'm going to need acts to book." He turned to face her fully, his eyes intense in the soft lighting. "And I already know exactly who I want as my first headliner."

The words struck her with surprising force. He wasn't just supporting her dream. He was tying his new career to it.

"You'd do that?" she whispered.

"I'd rather bet on you than play it safe."

Her eyes filled with tears. All week, she'd been terrified that choosing to be herself meant losing everything. But Jerome was choosing her. Choosing them. Choosing to build something real together.

"Yes," she said, and the word came out fierce and certain. "God, yes."

He leaned forward and kissed her, and this time there was nothing tentative about it. This was a promise, a commitment, a celebration of everything they'd discovered about themselves and each other.

When they finally broke apart, Jerome's smile was pure mischief.

"So," he said with a smile that tickled the corner of his eyelids. "Want to start a riot?"

About the author

I'm J.D. Harbor, a romance novelist drawn to love stories set on the high seas. A former military photojournalist, I found my writing voice capturing real-life moments in the field. Now, I craft tales of connection, adventure, and self-discovery aboard cruise ships.

The RomantiSea Serenades began with the interconnected duet of Emerald Tide and Sapphire Seas, companion novels with a shared love story between them. It has since expanded with two standalone novellas and my second interconnected duet, Scarlet Wave and Golden Shores. These stories are inspired by my own love story and the magic of love unfolding when least expected.

Originally from Utah, I now live in Central Florida with my wife and two kids, always dreaming up our next adventure on the open water. I believe the best love stories begin with self-discovery—because only when we truly know ourselves can we fully open our hearts to love.

Emerald Tide & Sapphire Seas

Available Now

Aidan's spent years carrying everyone else's expectations. Harper's built the perfect career that's slowly suffocating her soul. When they both end up on a singles cruise they never wanted to take, the last thing either expects is to find exactly what they've been missing.

He's all quiet loyalty and hidden longing. She's bright ambition wrapped around deep exhaustion. But somewhere between sunrise conversations and stolen moments, they realize that sometimes you have to drift away from shore to discover who you really are.

His story. Her story. One life-changing voyage.

Emerald Tide reveals his journey as a man torn between duty and dreams finally chooses himself. Sapphire Seas shows her path as a burned-out perfectionist learns that the best success stories aren't always the ones that look good on paper.

Ready to set sail? These full-length companion novels will sweep you away on a romance that proves the most beautiful destinations are the ones you never planned to reach.

RomantiSea Serenades: Where voyages of holding on and letting go find safe harbor.

Scarlet Wave & Golden Shores

Available Now

Scarlet's got the perfect life on paper, but she's drowning in her own success. Jerry lives for duty and his two sons, convinced that good fathers don't get to want anything for themselves. Neither planned to board a singles cruise, and they definitely didn't plan to fall for each other.

She's all sharp wit and polished control. He's quiet strength and hidden vulnerability. But somewhere between paddleboard disasters and late night heart-to-hearts, they discover that the best connections happen when you stop trying to stay afloat on your own.

Ready to dive in? This isn't just another shipboard romance. It's one epic love story that'll make waves in your heart.

Two perspectives. One unforgettable romance.

Scarlet Wave gives you her side as a burned out professional learns to sea life differently. Golden Shores shows his journey as a single dad discovers that love doesn't require perfection.

Get the complete story across two full-length companion novels. Trust me, you'll want to stay anchored to this romance from start to finish.

RomantiSea Serenades: Where solo journeys become shared memories.

www.ingramcontent.com/pod-product-compliance
Lightning Source LLC
LaVergne TN
LVHW021225080526
838199LV00089B/5827